Happy Ever After at Samphire Bay

Sasha Morgan lives in a village by the coast in Lancashire with her husband and has one grown up son. She writes mainly contemporary fiction, her previous series having a touch of 'spice', probably due to all the Jilly Cooper novels she read as a teenager! Besides writing, Sasha loves drinking wine, country walks and curling up with a good book.

Also by Sasha Morgan

Lilacwell Village

Escape to Lilacwell
Return to Lilacwell
Together in Lilacwell

Samphire Bay Village

Second Chances at Samphire Bay
A New Arrival at Samphire Bay
Happy Ever After at Samphire Bay

Sasha Morgan

Happy Ever After *at* Samphire Bay

First published in the United Kingdom in 2026 by

Canelo, an imprint of
Canelo Digital Publishing Limited,
20 Vauxhall Bridge Road,
London SW1V 2SA
United Kingdom

A Penguin Random House Company
The authorised representative in the EEA is Dorling Kindersley Verlag GmbH.
Arnulfstr. 124, 80636 Munich, Germany

Copyright © Sasha Morgan 2026

The moral right of Sasha Morgan to be identified as the creator of this work has been asserted in accordance with the Copyright, Designs and Patents Act, 1988.
All rights reserved. No part of this publication may be reproduced or transmitted in any form or by any means, electronic or mechanical, including photocopy, recording, or any information storage and retrieval system, without permission in writing from the publisher.
No part of this book may be used or reproduced in any manner for the purpose of training artificial intelligence technologies or systems. In accordance with Article 4(3) of the DSM Directive 2019/790, Canelo expressly reserves this work from the text and data mining exception.

A CIP catalogue record for this book is available from the British Library.

ISBN 9 781 80436 935 7

This book is a work of fiction. Names, characters, businesses, organizations, places and events are either the product of the author's imagination or are used fictitiously. Any resemblance to actual persons, living or dead, events or locales is entirely coincidental.

Printed and bound in Great Britain by Clays Ltd, Elcograf S.p.A.

Look for more great books at
www.canelo.co | www.dk.com

For Damon, Len and Wicklow, my little family in Dubai.

Chapter 1

'Thank you so much, Doctor O'Hara,' said the frail, old lady, fractured arm in a sling.

Tara smiled and nodded. 'Take care, Doris, and remember, no going out without assistance – at least for the next few weeks.'

Sighing with relief that she'd finally finished her shift, Tara made her way off the ward.

On the drive home, Tara's mood was reflective. Everything was getting harder. *Life* was getting harder. First, it was the general stress and pressure of her job – being a doctor on an A&E ward was certainly taking its toll. Home life wasn't much of an improvement; being in her mid-thirties and single wasn't a comforting prospect. Richard, her now ex-husband, had cleared off with his dental assistant Melissa, leaving her to tackle raising their fourteen-year-old son, Calum, with the usual grief teenagers bring their parents. It cut deep that Richard, although seven years her senior and in his early forties, had left her for a much younger woman in her mid-twenties.

Often, Tara would picture Richard and Melissa tucked up nicely in their new detached, state-of-the-art house, raking in a fortune from his dental practice, whilst she was left abandoned after fourteen years of marriage to cope with working full time and bringing up Calum.

It didn't help that their son seemed to blame her for the split either. The look of contempt he often threw her way was getting tiring now, as was the constant comparison to Melissa, his younger stepmother.

'Mel's a good laugh,' he'd gloat. 'She's got time for me, really listens,' he'd chide.

Then why not live with them? Tara was so tempted to snipe back but never did. She'd hate to lose her son. Richard had chosen the easy life, one that meant he could live exactly as he wanted. He earned a fortune and spent it on his glamorous new wife. He didn't need to be bogged down with the everyday hassle of a teenage son who moaned, criticised, played music too loud, stayed out late and persistently expected lifts everywhere. No, that was Tara's job, apparently. Richard just threw money at Calum to ease his conscience and saw him every other weekend. Job done.

As she pulled into the drive, Tara surveyed the beautiful Georgian house before her. It had been a family home since Calum was a toddler. Happy memories flooded her, way back to the very first time she and Richard had clapped eyes on it. It had been Richard who had spotted the house in the estate agent's window. Pulling her towards him, he pointed it out.

'Look at that,' he'd said in awe.

Tara, too, had been smitten with this real Georgian gem, set proudly on a leafy lane in Lancaster. It was a large, detached property made of white stone, and had two matching pillars either side of the front door. It had symmetrical sash windows, a hipped roof and wouldn't have looked out of place in a period drama. Inside was just as impressive, with its large reception rooms and stunning open-plan kitchen overlooking a huge, landscaped garden. There was plenty of entertaining space, which Tara and Richard had made good use of. They'd often hosted dinner parties with close friends or held family gatherings. She cast her mind back to barbeques in the garden, Richard playing football with Calum as she fussed over the grill; Saturday nights when they shared takeaways, huddled up together in front of the TV; even romantic suppers in the formal dining room when Calum had stayed over at a friend's house.

Then earlier memories shot into focus, like when they'd first stepped foot into the spacious hall, with its black-and-white chequered tiled floor and glimmering glass chandelier. They'd turned to face each other, trying not to radiate big beaming smiles in front of the estate agent. Richard, ever mindful of money, had given her strict instructions beforehand.

'Don't let the agent know you like it. Play it down,' he'd told her.

It was hard though, when both of them had instantly fallen in love with it.

In the end Richard had (reluctantly) offered the asking price. They had been elated when the estate agent handed the keys over. Their little family of three had stood patiently on the front step, eagerly waiting to enter their new home. Richard turned the key and in they went, their squeals of delight echoing around the large, empty hall. Once Calum had managed to climb the stairs, one hand clasping each spindle on the banister, the other in Tara's tight grip, he'd chosen his bedroom.

'Good choice, son,' said Richard, smiling in approval.

Calum had picked the room next to their master bedroom, overlooking the rear garden and orchard.

Now, as Tara opened the same front door, it was a very different story. No squeals of delight echoing around the hall, only a sad, empty silence. Boxes lay everywhere, filled with her and Calum's belongings, ready for the removal van. Richard's belongings had long since gone. Despite Tara's valiant attempts to keep the family home, it had to go. No way could she afford the mortgage on it, and absolutely *no way* was Richard going to contribute towards it either. In fact, Richard had made it blatantly clear just how much he actually was prepared to contribute. Nothing, if he had his way. Not only had it been up to Tara to fight for her and Calum's family home, but for substantial maintenance too. The first she'd been unsuccessful with, the second was an ongoing battle.

The injustice of it all still stung Tara. Especially given what she'd sacrificed. She was the one who had put her career on hold, while Richard had built up a successful, thriving practice. It was Tara who had been constantly there for Calum, attending football matches, school productions and parents' evenings, while Richard had poured more time, energy and money into his business.

What hurt Tara the most was Richard's treatment of their son. The blasé way he went in and out of his life. Yes, she accepted that she and him were never going to be friends, but Calum was the innocent in all this. The only person Richard had any real time for was his new wife. Although Calum seemed to enjoy staying with them, it was only every other weekend. This, to Tara, was grossly inadequate, given they didn't live that far away. She could only assume Melissa was behind it all, wanting at least one child-free weekend.

So, here they were, all packed up. Their possessions neatly boxed away, ready and waiting to be carted to another place. Their next home. This was the only thing that was keeping Tara going. She had recently bought a fabulous apartment in Samphire Bay. The location had long been a favourite of hers. The Lancashire village of Samphire Bay sat nestled just beneath the border to Cumbria, offering sheltered walks along limestone paths and amongst woodland, leading to open views of sandy beaches and glittering water. It was an intriguing and unusual place, with a windswept peninsula between the mouth of the river and bay, which at times was cut off by the tide. It had had a lot of coverage in the press several months ago, as the famous actor-cum-director, Felix Paschal, had bought the huge art deco house there.

Tara's apartment was one of a few that had been renovated from an old country house. The grand Victorian building looked most imposing, standing proudly flanked by tall fir trees. An 'Augusta House' sign hung from the cast iron gates by the entrance, which was operated by each resident's fob. It was all very sleek, classy and secure. The apartment had two decently sized bedrooms and a small balcony with a stunning view of the bay. Instinctively, Tara knew it was the place for her and Calum. What they lacked in garden the scenery made up for. In a nutshell, it was perfect. A fresh start.

'Hi, Calum, I'm home!' Tara shouted up the stairs. She could hear his music playing. It soon turned off and Calum came bounding down.

'Hi, Mum. What's for tea? I'm starving,' he groaned.

Tara smiled to herself. He was always starving, constantly eating. Mind you, she thought, he was definitely growing. Puberty had well and truly kicked in, giving her son a healthy appetite, as well as attitude. It was Friday, what the hell.

'Fancy a takeaway?' she asked, knowing full well what the answer would be.

'Result!' cheered Calum, giving her a high-five.

Tara loved this interaction, the easy way they rubbed along, when he wasn't being a difficult teenager. She knew he had reservations about leaving his childhood home, but she'd sold the new apartment in Samphire Bay very well to him. She'd even relented and allocated him the best bedroom with the balcony and view. It would be worth it though, anything to make their move as seamless as possible.

Chapter 2

For the last time ever, Robin locked the door behind him. That was it. The end of an era. The apartment was the first home he'd bought and he'd been immensely proud of it. Although he hadn't exactly put his stamp on it, never having had time to decorate, he'd still grown extremely fond of it. Still, Robin was glad to be going. Onwards and upwards. He was relocating to his girlfriend's, Jasmine, who had an old fisherman's cottage on the coastal path.

Having moved to Samphire Bay when he was seventeen from north London, Robin had fallen in love with the place immediately. This secluded village, with such spectacular scenery and beautiful bay, had enchanted him from day one. He'd also formed roots with the people living in Samphire Bay, particularly his best friend, Jack Knowles. He and Jack had hit it off straight away. Together, the two of them had been inseparable as teenagers. They'd had a magical time, partying on the beach, dancing under the stars and skinny dipping in the sea.

Robin and Jack, although still close and even working together now as building renovators, were opposites. Whereas Robin was dark and swarthy-looking, Jack was blond and had an almost boyish appearance. Robin was the quieter, more reserved of the two. Jack, however, lived up to his 'Jack the Lad' reputation. He drifted in and out of relationships. Apparently, he now had his eye on a woman he'd just recently met.

After Jack had an accident on the building site and cut his hand, Robin had rushed him to A&E. Little did Jack know that the doctor who'd caught his attention at the hospital was the very new owner of Robin's flat. However, Robin had kept this information to himself. Knowing how his best mate operated, he preferred to have the sale of his flat nicely in the bag before Jack bulldozed in feet first. Yes, definitely best to surprise him with the news, once everything had gone through. And now it had.

As Robin drove to the exit, he stopped and glanced back up at the elegant Victorian building. Turning, he drummed his fingers on the steering wheel and waited for the gates to open, then sped off to his new home.

Jasmine was resting with her feet up when Robin arrived. She'd spent all morning stencilling the nursery and was in need of a well-earned rest.

'Hi,' he called, entering the lounge. He kissed her forehead then sat beside her on the sofa.

'Everything OK?' she asked.

'Yep. All done. The flat is completely empty and, as of tomorrow, will officially no longer be mine.' He gave a happy sigh, glad the whole process was finally completed. He could now dedicate all his time and energy on their growing family.

He and Jasmine were expecting twins, which were due in August, just three months away. On the whole they were pretty well prepared. The pregnancy had come as a bit of a shock, and on learning it was twins, even more so. True to form, Jasmine had taken it in her stride. She was pragmatic and very level-headed. But then, she'd had to be. The poor girl had been made a widow at twenty-nine and as a result had chosen to move to Samphire Bay, restoring the old cottage they both lived in.

It was Robin who had given Jasmine the help she'd needed back then when they were neighbours. He and Jack had originally wanted to buy both adjoining cottages as a renovation project. They'd had visions of knocking through and creating a real spectacular detached property. However, they'd only managed to secure one. The owner of the cottages, an older lady called Bunty, had soon warmed to Jasmine and sold the other cottage to her. The two were now close friends.

Jasmine had fitted into Samphire Bay seamlessly and was regarded as 'one of them'. It was Jasmine who had helped Bunty trace an old flame from the past, Perry, and to everyone's delight, they had recently married. In fact, Bunty and Perry now lived next door, Bunty having bought back the cottage she'd sold to Robin and Jack after they had finished renovating it. She had previously lived in the art deco house on the peninsula, which was now occupied by Felix Paschal.

So, Samphire Bay was a place filled with people who actually *knew* each other. It was a hidden jewel, tucked neatly away on the north-west Lancashire coastline. Little wonder Robin didn't want to leave. No, he was more than happy to move into Jasmine's house and make it their family home.

'I've finished the nursery, by the way,' said Jasmine, rather pleased with herself.

'Great, I'll take a look,' replied Robin, then looked at her seriously. 'Don't do any more though, Jas,' he told her. 'You ought to be resting.'

'I'm fine,' Jasmine laughed, touched by his concern.

'No, really, don't do anything else,' insisted Robin.

'OK.' She shrugged, then turned to him with a sweet smile. 'Make us a cuppa, will you?'

'No problem.' He shot up to put the kettle on, making Jasmine grin to herself. She could get used to this, she thought wryly. Suddenly she felt movement in her swollen belly. The twins were on the move – again. Last night she'd hardly slept. It amazed her at seeing a bulge poke out from her stretched skin every now and then. It was incredible to think there were two tiny human beings inside her. Mind-blowing, really. She gently rubbed her abdomen.

'You all right in there?' she asked softly.

As if answering her, an elbow pushed up, followed by a foot. Jasmine took a deep breath in, then breathed out slowly. Something told her she'd be meeting them before August.

Next door, Bunty and Perry were still glowing from their honeymoon. Perry, having been a sailor in his day, had organised a luxury yacht cruise in St. Tropez. It had been an utterly enchanting time for them. Neither had known such lavishness. The yacht had six cabins, housing up to twelve guests, so it wasn't too overcrowded and created a more intimate experience. They'd had everything they could have wished for: a spa pool, cinema, beauty salon, gymnasium (not that they made use of that), a private deck and al-fresco dining area. They had anchored in superb landscapes and, as Perry had said, 'The sea remains the best way to reach St. Tropez. It avoids countless hours in traffic.' He'd been right. The captain had stopped at St. Tropez's most famous beach spots, and a village where Bunty and Perry had strolled around picturesque streets.

The newly-weds had enjoyed sunsets over the *Baie des Milliardaires*, where a verdant forest stood alongside deluxe properties.

'Give me our cottage any day,' remarked Bunty as the two had gazed out at the mansions sparkling in the sun.

'Absolutely,' agreed Perry.

The couple returned home fully refreshed, with golden tans and as loved-up as ever. As Jasmine had commented, it was lovely to see an older couple enjoying their best life. It restored faith in human nature to see two senior people, in the autumn of their lives, so completely happy and content. It had taken a while to get there though, having been separated many years ago, but they had finally made it.

'Well, Mrs Scholar, how does it feel to be back home?' said Perry with a grin.

'It feels marvellous,' replied Bunty, taking a good look around her beloved cottage. Whilst she'd thoroughly enjoyed sailing on the luxury yacht, with all its glamourous trappings, there was no place like home.

Chapter 3

Jack was relishing his morning run on the beach. It had always been his regular routine when younger, but less so as he'd got older. The property renovation business, which he'd formed with Robin, had completely taken over, and it was ironic that they should be at their busiest when he'd had to take a break to recover from his injury.

Jack had been installing the windows on their latest project when he'd tripped and fallen, causing the glazing to smash and cut his hand. After a rush to A&E and several stitches later, the doctor had advised he keep his injury clean and rest for a few days. The trouble was, Jack didn't really do resting. He was extremely active and perpetually on the go.

Having initially been the driving force behind the business, Jack had always pushed for the bigger, more ambitious developments. Sure, Robin was every bit as skilled a worker, but it was Jack who had had his sights set on the warehouse by the quay in Lancaster. As soon as the property went on the market, he'd seen its potential. It was huge, in an excellent location and could, with the vision he and Robin shared, be converted into apartments. After he'd managed to convince Robin, they had approached the bank with their proposition. They pitched a detailed plan of budgets, forecasts and profits, which had impressed the bank manager into giving them the loan they'd needed. Renovating the quayside warehouse was by far their biggest venture yet, and unfortunately, the worst timed.

As Robin would soon be needing paternity leave once his twins were born and Jack had to rest his injured hand, the two had decided to employ a small team of builders to help keep the renovation on track. Being in the trade for so long had meant they had connections and were able to get a good, reliable group of workers together. So, to some extent, the pressure had eased, but it was still leaving Jack feeling somewhat restless.

In an attempt to keep occupied, he had started his mornings with a good jog on the beach. It was proving to be beneficial, running off all that energy, giving himself a real blast of fresh air. All the exercise had pumped up his endorphin levels, leaving him in an optimistic mindset for the rest of the day.

Slowing down by the water's edge, he took in great gulps of air. He cast his eyes over his hand, which still throbbed slightly with pain. He assessed the neat row of stitches and admired the doctor's handiwork. Not as much as he'd admired the doctor though, he smirked to himself. Yes, true to form, Jack had *almost* seized an opportunity there.

The very attractive red-haired, slim doctor wearing royal blue scrubs had immediately taken his mind off the searing pain from his cut. Jack, being Jack, would have had the brass neck to ask her out there and then, but had held back. She was concentrating on stitching him up after all, and then, just as he was about to chat her up, a pager bleeped, sending her scurrying off. Damn, thought Jack, but even he conceded that this very pretty doctor did have far more pressing matters. Still, he knew where to find her, didn't he?

He took another lungful of the fresh sea air, then bent down to pick some samphire growing in the wet sand. Not only was he active, Jack also believed in eating well and looking after his body. Samphire, which grew in abundance here, hence its namesake, was an excellent source of vitamins and minerals. He often sautéed it with butter and added garlic or red pepper flakes. Besides being a very gifted building renovator, Jack was also an extremely good cook. He loved pottering in the kitchen, devising new recipes to try out and taste. He also loved cooking for other people, whether it be dinner parties for friends or candle-lit meals for girlfriends. But those occasions, just like his previous morning runs, had ceased to exist too of late.

In his quieter moments he did worry about how his life was unfolding – all work and no play. This was a far cry from Jack's former life, before he'd been committed to an ever-growing business. The old Jack had been full of bonhomie, raring to get out and socialise. He'd had a string (a long string) of doting girlfriends, but Jack had tended to use workload as an excuse to end his relationships. Now it was true; so true he wasn't even forming any. This wasn't due to lack of interest – far from it. His good looks had turned many a woman's head. With his short blond hair and sparkling blue eyes, he looked like a young Ewan McGregor. No, he simply hadn't found the time to plough into a relationship. Perhaps having some time off work lately had made him reassess his life, given him the space to consider what he was missing out on. Look at Robin, he managed his work-life balance well, didn't he?

Jack made his way back home, only a short walk down the beach, turning into a cove on the hillside. His house was his absolute pride and joy – and rightly so. Aptly named 'The Cove', it had a chalet vibe, made of large glass windows and plenty of wood with steps leading to a wraparound sundeck to take in the sea views, and had an outdoor shower and hot tub. Artfully shaped to echo and enhance the hillside setting made it a real unique build. It had been designed by a crack team with experience in travel, construction and interior design; mainly himself, his architect dad and interior designer sister. Building the house had been a family affair, and as heartfelt appreciation for their contribution, Jack had declared that it belonged to them all. His sister and her family holidayed there often, and his parents regularly visited on weekends.

Pounding up the wooden steps, Jack opened the large glass door and made his way into the open-plan main living area, consisting of a kitchen-diner and lounge. He washed the samphire in the sink and put it in the fridge to cook later. His kitchen units reflected the colours of nature outside, all dark blue gloss. He went up the stairs to a luxurious master bedroom, with a bespoke chunky wooden bed, to the en-suite with a walk-in shower. He badly needed to freshen up from his run. His sweat-stained T-shirt told him how out of shape he'd become.

As the hot, steamy jet of water sprayed over him, Jack contemplated further. No, he definitely *had* to make some changes. Number one: get a life. Make time for himself. Socialise with friends. Number two: get a girlfriend. He craved that one-on-one relationship that he'd so poorly lacked of late. The first he could do, of course he could.

It was just a matter of prioritising. The second, well…
Once again, that red-haired beauty flashed into his mind.
Now *that* he'd have to work on.

Chapter 4

'In your own time,' Calum said sarcastically, drumming his fingers against the overnight bag on his lap.

Tara took a deep breath and bit her tongue. She didn't want another argument just before dropping him off at his dad's. She started up the car and tried to stay calm. It was hard as Calum chirped away, saying how he was looking forward to seeing his dad and Melissa. Tara gripped the steering wheel tightly, gritting her teeth.

'What have you got planned?' she asked with forced politeness.

'We're going bowling.'

'Oh, right.' How many times had Richard refused to go out with them? Always complaining about how tired he was. More resentment started to flare up inside her. She took another deep breath.

'What's up?' asked Calum sharply, turning his head to look at her.

'Nothing. Tired, that's all.'

'Huh, what do you expect when you're at work all the time?' he retorted.

Unbelievable.

Tara's patience snapped.

'And why's that, Calum?' she fired back, taking him by surprise. 'Somebody has to bring home the bacon.'

'Sor-ry,' was his reply, dripping in scorn.

The rest of the journey was filled with stony silence – the very last thing she wanted before leaving him at his dad's. It didn't help seeing him sit up with excitement whilst pulling into the cul-de-sac of Bowland Rise, a newly built housing estate on the edge of Lancaster that boasted large, detached houses with views of the Bowland Fells.

'They've got a new fifty-inch plasma TV with surround sound. We're watching the new Bond film tonight,' he gloated.

'Lovely.'

'Right, see ya!' He shot out of the car to be greeted by Richard and Melissa at the front door. They looked like the perfect couple, then the perfect family when Calum joined them. Richard waved courteously at her. Tara nodded her head back civilly. She cast her eyes over Melissa standing beside him, one arm wrapped round his waist, staking possession. She was welcome to him. There was no backwards glance from Calum. The door slammed shut.

She took a moment to look at the big, executive house. It must have cost a fortune, but there was no accounting for taste, with its white, plastic doors, windows and flat-roofed conservatory plonked clumsily at the end. A far cry from the classy Georgian home they'd once shared. Tara sighed and set off back.

She was spending the weekend moving into her apartment in Samphire Bay. Tara had wanted to share the experience with Calum, but it had been Richard's turn to have him and he refused any flexibility. All her and Calum's belongings were stacked ready and waiting for the removal van, which was due to arrive within an hour. This gave Tara one last chance to say farewell to her beloved house. Entering each room, she glanced around for the last time and mentally said goodbye to each one. She didn't bother with the bedroom she'd shared with Richard. In fact, she was leaving behind the huge sleigh bed she'd shared with him too. Tara had refused point blank to touch the bed once Richard had left. She'd moved bedrooms and bought fresh furniture.

The main thing Tara was going to miss was the garden. She'd loved spending time out there, finding it very therapeutic, digging over the soil and planting fresh bulbs every year. Now she'd have to make do with a few potted plants on the balcony.

Still, the apartment was *theirs*. Hers and Calum's. A sanctuary where no one could come in, take over or abandon them. It was just them. Though, as things stood, she wasn't looking forward too much to a future with Calum and his mood swings.

Tara longed for the days when they'd been good buddies. She knew it was his hormones that made him the way he was at the moment, but she was convinced that the situation with Richard really wasn't helping. Calum had been unsettled by having to move from his family home. She also knew he missed his dad, only seeing him every other weekend. It was inevitable that Tara would be the punching bag for his emotions, as she was the one with him most of the time. All this only added to her state of mind – that life was too hard. Working full time really took it out of her, especially given what she did.

Fortunately her solicitor, Claire, was a good friend she had met at university. When Claire had represented her through the divorce, she had been at pains to persuade Tara to settle for a more realistic consent order, especially where maintenance was concerned. In Claire's opinion, Richard had basically got away scot-free.

'You're letting him get away with murder!' she'd exclaimed, wide-eyed in shock when Tara had calmly told her what she and Richard had agreed. But it was no use. No matter how hard Claire had tried to make Tara see sense, she simply shrugged.

'I just want rid of him. I can provide for myself,' she replied, almost in defeat. At the time this was true. She *did* want rid of Richard, but now she appreciated how she still needed his real input as a father to Calum, and that meant giving proper maintenance for him. It wasn't just Tara's responsibility to provide for their son, which up to now, it pretty much had been. Now, in the aftermath, when all the dust had settled from the contentious divorce, Tara realised just how much she had sacrificed. And it was about to change. She'd contacted Claire again, this time meaning business.

'It's not too late. I'm just glad you're doing something about it,' Claire told her firmly. She then promptly applied to the county court for a revised maintenance order, acting swiftly in case Tara changed her mind. It had grieved her watching Tara suffer the way she had, and she felt totally frustrated not being able to fight for a much better financial deal. Claire was used to wringing every last drop out of her clients' spouses, ensuring them full financial security. In Tara's case, the rich husband had walked away fully intact. In fact, he was actually going to make a profit from the sale of their beautiful family home. On top of that, he had speedily remarried and bought another big house for his new wife. The injustice of it all went against the grain for Claire. It just wasn't fair. Richard had taken advantage of Tara's vulnerability, wearing her down so there'd been no fight left in her.

Most of all, Claire knew that at the core of Tara's feelings lay humiliation, despite Claire's reassurance that it was *Richard* who ought to be embarrassed by his behaviour. After a few glasses of wine, Tara had once disclosed just how much her confidence had been knocked. Hearing this had sickened Claire. How could he do this to her beautiful, intelligent, fun-loving friend? Richard had simply sapped the life out of Tara, and she hated him for it. For Claire, fighting him for every penny she could get was not just a professional duty; it was personal. And she was going for the jugular.

So, with all this going on in the background, Tara was finally seeking closure with the house that had been her home for the past fourteen years.

Out of the bedroom window, she saw the removal van pull up. She quickly ran down the stairs and opened the front door.

'All set, love?' said a cheery chap dressed in overalls.

'As much as I'll ever be,' replied a subdued Tara.

Chapter 5

Jack sat at his kitchen table beside Robin, leaning over to study the interior layout draft for the warehouse renovation. The idea was to turn it into six apartments, and the initial outline had been approved in principle by the council, but now they had to submit a more detailed plan. Both had been originally tempted to go for seven apartments, there was enough room, but each one would have to be slightly smaller. Jack and Robin wanted to create something special, not mediocre. That meant having spacious rooms, capturing the views of the city skyline and quayside wherever possible. They intended to kit them out with top-quality fittings, including high spec kitchens and bathrooms.

They had hired an architect to design and reconfigure the internal walls and were giving the plans one last look over before presenting them to the planning department.

'Well, it all looks good to me,' concluded Robin after he finished scanning the draft paper roll.

'Yeah, me too,' agreed Jack with satisfaction. He was very happy with the architect's work. He, more than Robin, had liaised with her, given she was his dad's business partner. Jack had been reluctant to involve his father in this project, knowing how they'd disagreed so much when working on his house build. The trouble was, as his mother was fond of stating, he and his dad were too alike. Both had strong opinions and were keen to express them. It didn't do when those opinions clashed. So, the co-founder of his dad's company had given them the assistance they'd needed.

The renovation so far was still on track. The small group of builders put together after Jack's accident had come up trumps. The roof had been completely replaced and all window frames and glazing had been installed, making the building watertight. Now it was all internal work which, thankfully, wasn't weather reliant.

It was early evening and a deep pink sunset was flooding the bay. Robin glanced out of the large glass window to admire it.

'Fancy a beer?' asked Jack, getting up and heading for the fridge.

'No, thanks, better get back,' replied Robin.

Jack shrugged and took out a single bottle, hiding his disappointment. He'd wanted to chat to his best mate over a bottle of lager. These days all they managed to talk about was work, work, work.

'Jasmine will be waiting,' explained Robin.

'No doubt with a lovely supper cooked for you too.' Jack smiled, envying his friend.

Robin smiled in reply, then added, 'Come along, you're more than welcome.'

However tempting it was, Jack politely refused. 'No, thanks. You get yourself home, mate. Have a good evening.' He lifted his bottle in salute.

'Cheers, see you tomorrow,' said Robin, and made his way out.

Jack plonked himself down at the table and necked back his beer. This was the time he hated the most – evenings alone. After a hard day's work, when he'd slogged his guts out, he longed to relax – in company. He missed chatting about his day, just having that cosy, quiet time. He so envied Robin. Not that he begrudged his best friend's happiness, far from it. More than anyone, he knew how deserving both Robin and Jasmine were to have each other. But was it a crime to crave the same? All he wanted was a loving relationship too.

He knew full well what Robin's reaction would be, had he admitted this to him. He would've laughed and told him that he'd had more girlfriends than hot dinners. But they'd never been right, otherwise he wouldn't be on his own now, would he?

Sometimes it was hard pretending everything was hunky-dory. On the face of it, yes, it would appear so, but lately Jack had got to thinking. And his thoughts were beginning to pose questions, real questions about his lifestyle. It was all well and good having a thriving business and wonderful home, but not when you didn't have anyone to share it with. What was the point in earning good money if you could only enjoy it alone?

The days were becoming a monotonous routine for him – bed, work, bed. Gone were the days when he had partied, relishing life to the full. What the hell was happening to him? Shit, he wasn't going through some mid-life crisis, was he? He gulped back the rest of his beer. No, of course he wasn't, he told himself. Being thirty-two and single hardly constituted a mid-life crisis. Still, something wasn't right. He wasn't feeling himself lately and was at pains to know why. *Why* was he evaluating his own life this way? Maybe because he saw how settled Robin looked and dearly wanted the same. Yes, that must be it. It was hard not to covet what Robin had, a soulmate. Plus, he was about to start a family.

Jack looked around. Could he ever see a wife and children filling his home? Or would he be single for ever, rattling around this house solo? He pictured himself in years to come, shuffling about like some lonely, old hermit. Dear God.

Once more, his thoughts turned to that doctor he'd met in hospital. But who was he kidding? Even if she was available (and that was highly unlikely), how could he 'accidently' bump into her in the A&E department? He could hardly swan in and expect her to be available, or have the time for him, and that's if she even remembered him. No, he dully acknowledged, it was way too impractical. He'd have to try other avenues. Plenty more fish in the sea and all that.

Then a thought suddenly struck him.

It seemed the most logical solution, he wondered why he hadn't thought of it before. It was obvious! He wanted a partner and wasn't meeting one, so why not shop for one? Join a dating agency. The more he considered it, the more sense it made. An agency would cut out all the hassle, there'd be women lining up to meet him! With gusto, he grabbed his laptop and tapped away at the keyboard until a list of dating agencies in the area appeared on the screen. He clicked on the first link.

> Here at One-to-One, you can be assured of complete discretion. Our aim is to find your soulmate, your best friend, your happy-ever-after. Let us search for your perfect match and start enjoying life as a couple.

There it was again. *Soulmate*. That person to feel a deep, natural affinity for. He pressed the enrol button and began to fill in the questionnaire. Completing his personal details was the easy bit, then came the more searching questions. Are you more of an indoors or outdoors person? What do you like to do in your free time? What was the last book you really enjoyed? Who is the most fascinating person you've met?

Bloody hell, thought Jack, scratching his head. What happened to 'What's your tipple?' It all seemed pretty in depth to him. Then came the inevitable and arguably most crucial part of his profile: the photograph. He wouldn't struggle there. He was fortunately very photogenic. Jack did struggle however in picking the right one. Should he go for sporty, with him in his running gear, or something a little more formal? Then again, he didn't really do formal. In the end he settled for one of him with his family on holiday and zoomed in on himself with a head-and-shoulder shot. At least he looked natural. There, job done. All he needed to do now was pay the fee. His eyes widened at the price. Blimey, they certainly wanted their pound of flesh, didn't they? It better be worth it, he thought, tapping in his bank account details. Then, with a degree of hesitation, he pressed submit.

Chapter 6

Bunty and Perry were visiting Perry's stepdaughter, Emma. She lived with Felix in Bunty's former home, the huge, white art deco house on the peninsula. Last year, Emma had applied to become the housekeeper there, after Felix's PA had forced him into advertising the post. It was poor Jennifer who'd been expected to play hostess and cook, as well as attend to her usual admin duties. While being interviewed, Felix had recognised Emma as the woman who'd played the piano at the open day when he'd bought the house. The attraction between the two had been patently obvious for all to see, especially Felix's mother, Madeleine, who had predicted that the pretty, young housekeeper with long chestnut hair and plenty of spirit wouldn't stay the housekeeper for very long. She'd been proved right. Within a few months, Felix had well and truly fallen for Emma, and in return, Emma too was smitten with the handsome, dark-haired, olive-skinned actor.

Emma, besides being housekeeper, was also a talented singer and musician. Felix had arranged for her to sing the theme tune for the latest drama he had directed, *Lady Scarlett Investigates*. The filming had taken place at his home, it being the ideal location with the show set in the 1920s.

Initially, Perry had had reservations about the whole setup. Being a very protective father, he hadn't been too pleased to learn that Emma's employer had in fact turned into her boyfriend. It hadn't helped, either, that the man in question was the famous actor turned director Felix Paschal. In Perry's eyes, he worried that his daughter was just a passing fancy, to be discarded once the novelty wore off. But, thankfully, after meeting Felix and seeing the two together, Perry realised he was worrying unduly. It was plain to see that Felix adored Emma. It was also blatantly clear how happy Emma was too.

For Bunty, a trip back to her childhood home caused mixed emotions. It had taken some guts to put the place on the market, having lived there all her life. Every corner, nook and cranny held fond memories for her – well, almost. One particular incident on the sweeping staircase did not. Here her father had stood at the top, looking down dismissively on a young Perry, who definitely had not met his expectations. Because of Bunty's father, who refused to even acknowledge him, she and Perry had been cruelly separated. Bunty had been forced to see him in secret, which inevitably led to an ultimatum. Perry had, quite rightly, made a stand. It was him or her father. Bunty, always the dutiful daughter, had made the biggest mistake of her life and chosen the wrong man. She couldn't leave Daddy, he *needed* her, she'd pleaded, hoping to placate Perry. But no, Perry had exited her life and left Samphire Bay.

However, fate had played a part in reuniting the pair in later life. Jasmine, who had once lived on a narrowboat, had had contact with an older fellow sailor, named Perry, who'd owned a boat too. It later transpired that it was indeed the same Perry and Jasmine had persuaded Bunty to make contact. It was so the right move. This time she *had* made the right decision. Once the two reunited, they'd soon become inseparable and that Christmas Day saw them engaged to be married. The following spring in April, last month, they finally tied the knot.

Nobody more than Emma had been thrilled by her dad's second chance at love. As far as she was concerned, he'd suffered enough when her mum had died of breast cancer and she'd often encouraged him to 'get out there'. After over a decade, he was at last happy with another wife.

As Bunty and Perry pulled onto the driveway and made their way up the stone steps to the front entrance, Emma flung the doors open. Once inside, Bunty couldn't help skimming her eyes over the grand hall, taking in the high, cherry-yellow ceiling with glamorous lighting in gold leaf and chrome finishing, the full-length fan wall mirror and the curved staircase. The rooms leading off the hall had the typical art deco sunburst mantels above the doorframes and the light switches had the original brass cases. It was all so captivating and very fitting of the era it had been built. Oh, how she missed it!

'Hi!' Emma gushed, hugging each of them. It was so good to see the couple after their honeymoon. She eyed one, then the other. 'You're both looking well,' she commented.

'Married life obviously suits them,' said Felix, coming up from behind Emma. 'Hi, Perry.' He shook his hand, then kissed Bunty on her cheek. 'Bunty, you look as radiant as ever,' he grinned, making Bunty roll her eyes.

'Don't overdo it, darling,' she replied, making them all chuckle. Bunty was a hard nut to crack. Flattery would get this handsome famous actor nowhere. He was simply Emma's boyfriend to her, and Perry too for that matter.

'Come through. I'll make us drinks.' Emma ushered them into the impressive drawing room. The high dusky pink walls were covered with two elaborate mirrors and various water-coloured paintings in gold, ornate frames. Emma went to a retro glass drinks cabinet and began making them all cocktails while Bunty looked on with affection. How she'd loved that cabinet and made extremely good use of it! It had been a wrench to leave it behind, but the fixtures, fittings and art deco furniture were all included in the house sale. As a consolation, Robin and Jack had promised to keep their eyes open for a similar drinks cabinet in the house clearances they often attended.

'There you go.' Emma offered them all a drink on a silver tray.

'Oh, lovely. What are these?' asked Bunty, secretly craving just a stiff gin and tonic.

'Ever After Appletinis. I thought them very appropriate.' Emma smiled whilst Felix looked pensively at her. She turned and they locked eyes.

'I see,' replied Perry, taking everything in. Maybe there was to be another wedding in the future?

'Hmm, these are delicious,' remarked Bunty, a tad surprised at how much she did like them, then swiftly changed the subject. 'So, when is *Lady Scarlett Investigates* hitting our screens?' They all looked at Felix.

'Late summer apparently. The exact dates have yet to be finalised,' he answered.

'I can't wait,' gushed Emma. Not only was she super excited to see the drama, but also to hear her voice singing the opening theme tune. It had been a dream come true, knowing her voice was about to be heard by the nation, after years of her band trying to make it in the music business. She could still hardly believe it.

Perry smiled to himself. He too was elated for his daughter. He reflected on how unhappy Emma had been working as a bank clerk. The housekeeper position she'd taken had only meant to be a temporary thing until the band 'made it big'. Now look at her.

Chapter 7

Tara sat back in satisfaction and looked around their new apartment. She admired the high ceilings and cornices, loving the Gothic influences and intricately designed woodwork the large Victorian house had. Fortunately, the building had been renovated sympathetically to its original features. It was everything and more that she'd wanted, what *they* wanted. Calum had been in awe of his bedroom, thank goodness. Giving him the bedroom with the balcony had been a real deal breaker and well worth the sacrifice. Robin had even left the small bistro set for them, which was very kind of him. Yep, life was slowly on the up, she thought, so glad to have moved into a home she could call her very own. *Nothing* to do with that ex-husband of hers.

Then, just as she was basking in the contented glory, who should ring the flat's intercom? Why, Richard, of course, forever having a habit of sapping any of her positivity. He buzzed again impatiently. Tara smirked to herself, knowing how it must annoy him having to speak through an intercom to gain entrance into the Augusta House grounds. She pressed the button by her door.

'It's me,' said Richard somewhat petulantly.

'OK, come through,' replied Tara, still smirking. She saw the big cast iron gates open through the window and Richard's car drive in. Calum was in the passenger seat looking a tad sullen. Tara frowned, hoping everything was all right with him. Then they both got out and made their way towards the building, causing her to frown again. Why was Richard coming up too?

Something was afoot. Tara had detected a sense of foreboding in the air for some time now. A pattern gradually seemed to be forming, one that involved Richard's weekends. Calum had returned more subdued than normal lately. Tara didn't like it. Although she appreciated the free time to herself, another part of her resented the way Richard was starting to manipulate Calum, as if he was calling all the shots, dictating when and how long Calum was to stay at his. Richard had apparently requested to see Calum's form tutor at school, but Tara hadn't been told why. It all unnerved her. Now, watching him saunter into the building with Calum, she mentally prepared herself for the obvious confrontation that was about to follow. He might look casual and relaxed, but underneath she knew full well how determined and controlling Richard was. The cheery wave and warm smile he gave through the window meant nothing. He was transparent to her and Tara saw straight through his façade.

Answering the door, she told herself to stay cool and calm, no matter what he was about to throw at her. The fact Calum was with him told her he would be reasonable, to a degree, not wanting to cause too much of a scene with him about.

'Hello, Richard,' she said dully, opening the door, then smiled at Calum as he barged in.

'Hi, Mum,' he called over his shoulder, heading straight to his bedroom.

'Can I come in, Tara? There's something I need to discuss with you.'

Her heart sank. What bombshell was he about to drop? Tara nodded and stepped aside to let Richard enter. Already Calum had started playing his music.

'Come through,' she said. 'Do you want a drink?'

'Thanks.'

Richard sat awkwardly at the breakfast bar whilst Tara put the kettle on. She felt his eyes on her back, watching her every move. Turning, she placed a cup of coffee down on the bar before him. He coughed uncomfortably then began.

'Melissa and I are having a baby.' He paused to search her face for a reaction. There wasn't one. Tara just stared back, expressionless. 'I told Calum a short while ago and... Well, to be honest, I'm not sure how he feels about it.'

'Did you ask him?' she replied flatly.

'Yes, but he didn't really give a reply, just kind of grunted.'

Welcome to my world, was the reply Tara felt like giving. Clearly Calum hadn't jumped with elation at his father and stepmother's news. She must admit, it did come as a bit of a surprise, especially given the way both Richard and Melissa had initially been reluctant to spare time for Calum. That and the fact they were both so materialistic. They didn't strike her as the family type, more interested in ploughing their energies into the dental practice – and reaping its hefty profits.

Tara crossed her arms and continued to stare at her ex-husband. His hair was greying more at the temples. One or two wrinkles had appeared. And this was before a crying baby was about to keep him up all night. Oh dear, oh dear, she thought somewhat smugly.

Richard watched her scrutinise him and instantly read her mind. He hated the thought of his good looks fading. He hated the thought of growing old, especially when he had a new young wife to please, which was proving bloody difficult at the best of times – and this wasn't the best of times. For he, too, had been surprised. He always believed Melissa was on the same page as him, wanting a good social life, weekends away, foreign holidays, expensive hobbies and shopping sprees. Not nappy changing and play dates. Never before had she ever mentioned starting a family, otherwise he would've talked her out of it. But maybe clever Melissa understood him better than he'd understood her, because when she had announced her pregnancy – or rather, '*their* pregnancy' – she looked the epitome of happiness itself. He'd been shafted. This was *not* what he'd signed up for. But it was too late now. His beautiful, calculating wife had seen to that.

He weighed Tara up, only now appreciating what he'd actually had – an honest, hard-working woman and a great mum. He gave her an almost pleading look, willing her to give him some sort of reassurance.

'What exactly do you expect me to do, Richard?' Tara asked in a bored tone.

He blinked, not quite believing her cold attitude. 'I'd like you to talk to Calum for me. Make him understand he's still my main priority.'

'And is he?' she replied bluntly, making him flinch.

'Of course he is. I've tried spending more time with him, hoping he knows I'll always be there if he needs me. But…'

'But what?' Tara snapped impatiently, growing tired of listening to Richard's whiney voice.

'He doesn't want to talk about it. Refuses to acknowledge the fact he'll be a big brother.'

'Well, he's got time to adjust.' She shrugged her shoulders. 'I suggest you persevere. Just like I do.' She smiled politely. 'Now, if you don't mind, I'm expecting company,' she lied, eager to see the back of him.

'Oh, right,' he replied, somewhat deflated. On his way out he called, 'I'll see you next weekend, Calum!'

'Whatever,' came the reply.

Richard looked at Tara as though wanting support from Calum's blasé response. He didn't get any. She just stared him out.

'Well... I'd better get going,' he said dejectedly.

'Yes,' replied Tara, crossing her arms. 'Melissa will be waiting,' she added, smiling sweetly. Richard gulped. Tara resisted the urge to laugh out loud. 'Goodbye, Richard,' she said. And with that, she closed the door.

She looked towards Calum's bedroom and hesitated. Should she go in and speak to him? No, that was exactly what Richard wanted. She'd speak to their son when he was ready, in *his* time.

Chapter 8

Jack walked into the coffee shop and discreetly scanned the tables.

That must be her, he thought, noticing a woman with curly blonde hair sat alone by the bay window.

After registering with the dating agency and finding a match, the agency had exchanged more detailed profiles for the couple, so he'd learnt a little more about Sandy. Besides being an artist and having a fondness for travelling, she was a divorcee, had several nephews and nieces, was born in Australia and had a black belt in karate. Jack had been impressed.

He, in turn, had supplied further personal information about himself. He'd thought long and hard about how to strike the right tone, mindful of how well Sandy came across. He wanted to sound as interesting as she did, but found it difficult. To be fair, his first profile pretty much summed him up – he was thirty-two, a building renovator and looking for Miss Right. What more was there to say? He elaborated with a few white lies by exaggerating his globe-trotting. He invented a few 'backpacking' holidays and claimed to have worked as a lifeguard in an attempt to appear more interesting. Once again, Jack had doubted whether this online dating thing was really for him. But he'd committed to the agency, paid the registration fee and was damned if he'd fall at the first hurdle. Besides, seeing Sandy wave up at him from her table by the window helped him feel more optimistic.

'Hi, I sussed it was you by the way you were searching the room.' She held her hand out to shake.

'Hi, I'm Jack,' he replied, then immediately felt foolish for introducing himself unnecessarily. She obviously knew who he was.

'Sandy,' came the reply, making him feel better.

He was instantly struck by her confidence. Then another thought occurred to him. Was she used to this? How many other dates had she been on?

'I've not ordered yet,' she continued, pointing to the menu. 'Thought I'd wait for you.'

'Thanks.' He smiled and looked at the lunchtime specials. He didn't have much of an appetite. He was actually a tad nervous, which surprised him. Normally he wouldn't have any reservation on a first date, even a blind one, but somehow this was different. It just didn't seem natural.

'So, tell me about yourself,' Sandy said, a touch too loudly for Jack's liking. The couple sitting on the table next to them glanced over, obviously overhearing her and quickly gained interest.

He suddenly felt terribly self-conscious. He coughed and waited for them to turn away. Sandy seemed oblivious to it, elbows on the table, chin resting on her palms, waiting for an answer. He stalled further, before her raised eyebrows and big beam encouraged him to reply.

'To be honest, you already know most of it from my profile.' This caused exchanged smirks from the nosy couple. He cringed inside. 'I spend most of my time working, or drinking with my mates.' However true, he couldn't help but hear how lame this sounded. Deciding to change tack, he quickly asked, 'So, where in Australia were you born?'

'Mooloolaba.'

'Ah, the Sunshine Coast.' One of his friends had visited there and sent him a postcard once. Sandy's face lit up. 'You know it?'

'Err... Well, I've never been.'

'Oh,' she replied, deflated. Jack's stomach began to churn. What the hell was the matter with him?

'I think I'll just have a coffee,' he said, not wanting to risk eating.

'Right. Fine.' Sandy nodded, tight-lipped.

He hoped he hadn't offended her. To his relief the couple next to them got up and left, leaving them with a bit of space. He settled down once their drinks arrived.

'What does a pretty lady like you need to join a dating agency for?' Jack asked. He genuinely considered it a compliment. But judging by the look Sandy was giving him, he doubted she took it as such.

'I don't *need* to join an agency. I just prefer to.' She glared at him.

'I didn't mean—'

'Because I thought a dating agency would cut out the crap,' she interrupted in a harsh tone, once again causing a few turned heads.

Jack blinked. He was speechless.

'Look, Sandy, I really didn't mean to cause any offence,' he said in a low, hushed voice.

'None taken,' she said, clearly lying, then swivelled her head to look out of the window. This wasn't going to plan. Jack looked sexy and good fun on his profile. Sandy believed they'd have a lot in common, especially because he was as well travelled as her. But no, he was...

stilted, maybe a touch condescending? The comment on 'pretty ladies' *needing* to join a dating agency! Really? How patronising.

Jack coughed again, sensing the tension build. He'd make one last valiant effort, then balls to it.

'What have you got planned tonight?' he asked, deciding to take the bull by the horns. Maybe if they met on his territory, his local pub, things might be easier.

'I'm on another date.' She stared him out.

'Oh, I see.' Clearly he didn't. How many profiles had the agency thrown her way? He'd naturally assumed she would only be seeing one bloke at a time. He really was out of touch. Jack's doubts about the whole online dating scene were proving him right. It wasn't for him. It felt too forced.

'So, it's been nice meeting you… err… Jack,' she said, pretending to forget his name momentarily, 'but I've gotta go.' And with that she finished her coffee, scraped her chair back and practically marched out, leaving him somewhat rejected, and with the bill.

Jack sat back and sighed. That went well – not. A part of him wanted to email the dating agency and demand a refund. Then, all of a sudden, he saw the funny side. What could he write? It wasn't the agency's fault Sandy had taken the huff and walked out on him. He'd obviously said the wrong thing, albeit inadvertently. Better to just put it down to experience, but did he want to go through the whole thing again? No, he didn't. Perhaps if he hadn't had reservations in the first place, he might have given it another go, but, truth be told, his heart wasn't really in it.

Sipping his coffee, he looked through the window at the world going on outside. Was it just him, or did everybody seem to be in couples? Jack's gaze followed them, sauntering about, arms wrapped round each other, laughing while looking into each other's eyes. It pissed him off. He knew how resentful he was becoming and it scared him. It wasn't like him to feel this way. Just as he was about to finish his coffee and leave, his mobile rang. It was Robin.

'Hi, Rob.'

'Hi, you busy, mate?'

'Nah, just in town and about to set off home. Why?'

'Just thought I'd call round, if you're free?'

'Yeah, sure, give me half an hour.'

At least he had a good friend in Robin, thought Jack.

—

Robin had felt a little guilty the other night when he hadn't stayed at Jack's for a beer. He'd sensed that his mate might have needed some company, which then prompted him to think about Tara, the lady who'd bought his apartment. He had always intended to tell Jack that the doctor he'd been so attracted to at the hospital was in fact the new owner. Now, given that it had been a couple of weeks since she'd moved, he assumed the coast was clear. The last thing Robin wanted was for his mate to go bounding into her life before she'd settled in. Jack did have form. Although he was his best mate, Robin knew how he operated and in some way almost felt obliged, responsible even, because she'd bought his flat.

The two of them were sat outside on the decking, drinking bottles of beer, when Robin decided to tell him. Jack stopped mid-drink and blinked.

'What? You mean that gorgeous doctor has been here all this time, in Samphire Bay?'

'Well, only a couple of weeks, mate,' replied Robin.

Jack couldn't help but laugh at the irony. In those two weeks he'd joined a dating agency whilst the girl of his dreams had been yards away, literally.

'What are you laughing at?' Robin asked bemused.

'Nothing,' Jack said shaking his head. 'And I take it this Tara is single?'

'Divorced apparently. She has a son.'

The fact Tara was a mum didn't alter his attraction. If anything, it made him admire her more. It couldn't be easy being a single parent and managing to hold down a stressful career too. She was obviously a woman of substance.

'I see.' Jack nodded in contemplation. Well, well…

Chapter 9

Jasmine slowly and steadily made her way up the stairs. They seemed to be getting harder to climb, she thought, pausing for breath halfway. She finally reached the top when there was a knock at the back door. Typical. Refusing to go back down and answer it, she went into the bedroom and looked out of the window to see Bunty. Jasmine tapped on the glass and waved, mouthing for her to come in.

Moments later she heard Bunty huffing and puffing up the stairs too.

'Hi!' she called, meeting her on the landing. Bunty grinned.

'Hello, darling, how are you feeling?' Her eyes automatically homed in on Jasmine's large bump.

'Tired,' came the faint reply. Jasmine refrained from saying she was just about to have a lie down. Instead, she directed Bunty into the nursery, eager to show it off.

The walls were painted a warm cream, and a matching Roman blind hung in the window. Not knowing the sex of their babies, Robin and Jasmine had gone for a fresh, neutral shade, brightening the room up with vibrant accessories; a large multi-coloured rag rug lay on the wooden floor and cheerful nursery pictures dotted the walls, plus various soft toys sat waiting patiently on shelves.

'Oh, it's wonderful,' trilled Bunty, taking it all in. She walked over to the matching cots, stood side by side, and looked at Jasmine. 'Excited?' she asked.

'Yes, I'll be glad when they're here, safe and sound,' she replied, rubbing her swollen stomach.

'Of course you will.' Bunty assessed her friend. Although Jasmine was undoubtedly tired, she still glowed. Her blue eyes sparkled, her complexion was flawless and her blonde hair positively shone. Jasmine looked the picture of good health. 'Make the most of your free time,' Bunty advised, chuckling.

'Everyone keeps saying that,' said Jasmine, knowing how busy she was about to become as the mother of twins. But how was she supposed to sleep when she felt so uncomfortable? It was impossible to get in an easy position being the size she was. She was officially due in August, but had been advised to prepare herself for an earlier birth. It was very common for multiple births to arrive sooner than a single one. This hadn't come as a shock to Jasmine, who already felt like she was about to go into labour. Now, at this later stage in her pregnancy, she was being monitored extremely closely by the maternity clinic, not to mention Robin, who watched her every move. Jasmine's parents, too, often rang and visited, understandably so. But what she really craved was peace and quiet, to be left alone, calmly getting on with things, like she usually did.

There was no denying that Jasmine was a coper. After what life had thrown at her, she'd learnt to be. Even so, as Robin had pointed out, this was *their* pregnancy, not just hers. Yes, she was the one carrying the babies, but as their father, Robin couldn't wait to be hands-on once they were born.

'We're a family now,' he'd told her, 'It's you, me and our babies. That's what counts.'

Jasmine couldn't have wished for a more supportive, loving partner. He'd wanted to be married before the twins were born, but Jasmine didn't want a rushed wedding.

'Why not take our time after they're born?' she'd said. It seemed so pointless to her to have the pressure of a wedding on top of everything else. Robin had agreed, reluctantly. Secretly, Jasmine would be quite happy to have a low-key registry office affair, but knew damn well how that would go down – on all fronts. For a start, her mum would never forgive her, and Robin? Well, she couldn't deny him a big, fat wedding, could she? After all, he hadn't been married before, whereas she had…

Thoughts turned to her and Tom's wedding day. She really had had the full works there, a huge, traditional family wedding. For a moment her eyes misted over.

'You all right, darling?' Bunty asked, snapping Jasmine out of reverie.

'Hmm? Oh, yes… Sorry, I was miles away.'

'Come on, let's sit down. I'll pop the kettle on. You,' Bunty said and pointed at her, 'are going to put your feet up.'

For Jasmine, it was lovely having Bunty as a neighbour. Although there was such an age gap between them, it didn't stop them from being close friends. They shared the same sense of humour and Bunty often had Jasmine in peals of laughter. She was a gifted mimic, with an ear to imitate people's voices. She was also good fun. Last year, while still living in her old house, she held a dinner party and had requested formal dress. Bunty had worn one of her mother's old 1920s dresses, resembling a flapper girl, really getting into the spirit of things. Jasmine couldn't help but compare Bunty to her own mum; they were poles apart.

Once sat on the settee with her feet up, as ordered by Bunty, Jasmine closed her eyes and listened to her singing in the kitchen.

'...where babies float by, just counting their toes...'

Jasmine smiled to herself and drifted off into a peaceful nap.

-

Meanwhile, Robin was working flat-out at the warehouse. He was overseeing where a partition wall was to be erected when Jack joined him. Robin turned to face him with a smile.

'Hi, Rob, how's it going?'

'Everything's under control.' Robin nodded confidently, pleased to see his work mate.

'Good. I'm coming back to work,' Jack stated, looking around at the progress that'd been made since he'd damaged his hand.

'Sure?' said Robin.

'Yeah, my wound is healing nicely.' He lifted his hand for Robin to see the stitches that had neatly matted together. 'As long as I keep it clean, wear gloves, it should be fine.'

'Yes, as per the doctor's orders,' Robin said with a smirk. They exchanged knowing looks. 'Talking of which, have you made your move yet?'

Jack laughed, knowing full well what his friend was referring to.

'Give us a chance, mate,' he grinned. 'But I'll be on the case.' He winked, making Robin throw his head back and chuckle. Same old Jack.

Chapter 10

Tara was flicking through a magazine with her feet up for once. It was Saturday morning, Calum had stayed at his friend's the night before and she wasn't due on shift until the following afternoon.

Her peace and quiet was disrupted by a loud buzz from the intercom. Frowning, she looked out of the window to see Richard's car through the iron gates, waiting to be let in. She was half tempted to ignore him, but knew he'd be persistent. Bloody Richard. He'd obviously got the solicitor's letter. She braced herself for the onslaught. This time she was ready for him. This time she would not cave in.

She got up to answer the intercom. Cutting out the niceties, she pressed the button and said, 'It's open.' She stood by the door, waiting with a steely nerve for him to enter the building and stride down the corridor.

Moments later, he rammed on the front door, unnecessarily loud. Taking a deep breath, she opened it and looked him fully in the eye. He was incandescent with fury, clutching the letter in his hand.

'What the hell?' he raged, waving the paper in her face. Tara remained calm. 'We'd agreed everything! So why go back to court now?'

'Because, Richard, I've changed my mind,' she answered flatly.

'Why?' he spat. Tara turned her back on him and walked away, leaving the door open for him to follow. The last thing she needed was a showdown within earshot of the neighbours.

Richard stormed in, slamming the door behind him, making it rattle. Again, she counselled herself to stay composed, though her patience was reaching breaking point. More than anything, she was very aware of being alone in the apartment. She turned to face him.

'Why, Tara?' he demanded.

'I'm tired, Richard. I work every hour God sends at the hospital and I want more time. I want a *life*.'

'But... but...' he spluttered.

'No, Richard, no buts. You earn a fortune and it's time you contributed your fair share.' Tara folded her arms across her chest, subconsciously acting as a barrier between them.

'I do contribute.'

'Not enough and you know it.'

'It's not as if you're as poor as a church mouse, is it?' he spoke quietly, almost menacingly.

'You know damn well how hard I work.'

At least he has the grace to blush, she thought.

'All I know is that we were both happy with the arrangement... And now...' Then something dawned on him. Her friend was acting as her solicitor. 'Oh, I know what this is about. It's that stupid cow Claire, isn't it? She always did have it in for me.'

'No, this has come from *me*,' Tara replied, then added, 'although, yes, you're right about Claire. She does have it in for you.' She smiled sweetly, sending Richard's temper into orbit. He made a move towards her, then stopped in his tracks at the sight of her face. 'You come any nearer and you will so regret it,' she warned in a low, stern voice. 'Do you want to be dragged through the courts for assault too?'

This made him freeze. The stark reality of the situation finally struck home. If his reputation was tarnished, that would impact his professional life, not to mention how Melissa would react, or her family. He gulped. A film of moisture suddenly covered his skin.

'Tara, listen—' he tried to reason.

'No, you listen, Richard.' Her eyes sparked with anger. 'This is the last time you enter my home. In future, all correspondence will be through our solicitors. You can contact Calum directly.' Richard blinked, not quite believing his ears. 'I've nothing more to say to you, except leave.'

She walked towards the door and opened it. Richard slowly made his exit, shoulders drooping slightly. As he passed her, he made one last attempt to speak, but she immediately silenced him with her raised hand.

'Don't, Richard. Just don't.' She watched him slope down the corridor, very much the wounded soldier. What an absolute prick, she thought, then locked the door shut.

Trust Richard to ruin what precious little time she had to herself. She wasn't picking Calum up from his friend's house until later that day, so, determined not to waste the rest of the morning seething over her idiot ex-husband, Tara changed into her running gear. It had been ages since she'd gone out on a run and really stretched her legs.

Within ten minutes she sprinted out of the Augusta House grounds and made for the nearby woods that led onto the bay. It was a glorious route through the tall pine trees, jogging on soil covered with needles. She breathed in their musty scent, loving the dappled sunshine glowing gently through the branches. Finally the soil turned to sand as she came to a clearing. The bay was now in sight.

Tara stopped and took in a lungful of fresh air. She put a hand up to shield her eyes from the sun and surveyed the magnificent sight before her. How uplifting it was. The glittering turquoise water was enough to raise anyone's spirits. She'd so made the right move coming here.

Her gaze was drawn to the peninsula and the huge house on it, which was cut off by the tide at the moment. How lucky, thought Tara, wishing she could afford the same luxury, to be secluded from all and sundry twice a day. Then her eyes wandered to the soft white dunes covered in samphire. She squinted at seeing another runner, clearly in good shape as his toned body pounded along the sand. Then she watched with interest as he slowed down and stopped to pick some samphire. Tara remained discreet, the pine trees providing a cover. He seemed very preoccupied with his task, putting the samphire into a small plastic bag then stuffed it into his jogging bottoms' pocket. What a good idea, Tara thought, knowing how much goodness was packed into the small plant. Hmm, he obviously looks after himself. Her stare followed him as he set off running again, then she too set off, jogging down the beach at a reasonable distance behind him.

Inhaling the salty air and enjoying the sun on her face, she relished the exercise. All the while, the man in front of her thundered down the sand at high speed, oblivious to her in the rear distance. Then, to her surprise, he suddenly went left into a cove. Tara hadn't even known there was a cove here, it was so well tucked away.

Curiosity got the better of her and she took the same turning – but quickly halted when she realised what was there. A house. A beautiful, stunning beach house! She saw the man run up the wooden decking, up the steps two at a time, then enter it. Tara, not wanting to be seen, turned to run in the opposite direction, but not before edging closer to get a better look at what she'd discovered. What a fantastic home, she admired in awe. How she envied the owner of this house. It may not be on the peninsula with the seclusion she craved, but still, what an absolute gem it was, having the beach on your very own doorstep.

Tara set off again retracing her footsteps. Once she made it back to Augusta House, she felt totally rejuvenated, ready to take on the world – and Richard. Now she just grinned to herself at Richard's response to the solicitor's letter. He was about to get his just deserts, well overdue and well deserved.

Chapter 11

Jack narrowed his eyes for a better view outside. Who was that? He stood at the sink, pouring himself a glass of water after his run, when someone caught his attention from the kitchen window. He stopped short, focusing in on the red bobbed hair. It was her, Dr O'Hara. He blinked. Yes, he wasn't imagining it! Then, to his dismay, she turned to go.

Jack watched the back of her, appreciating the slim, svelte body moving with ease across the sand. Had she hung around, he'd have gone out to join her, invite her in, if she was so curious about his home. Hmm, it did give him food for thought though. Dr O'Hara was obviously a runner too. Had she been jogging behind him all the time on the beach? She must have been, but he hadn't seen her. Jack cursed the missed opportunity. Of all the bloody luck, to be totally oblivious of the very woman occupying his thoughts being there, right behind him.

All sorts of scenarios crossed his mind. He looked at his watch and made a note of the time: 11:40 a.m. Would she be there tomorrow, running on the beach at the same time? Was this a regular routine for her as well? He dearly hoped so.

Jack smiled. This was indeed welcome news. He saw an opening on the horizon. They had something in common – running – and he knew where to find her – the beach – and now he had an excuse to engage her in conversation

– his home. Who wouldn't be interested in exploring his impressive beach home? Many a time he'd been stopped by passers-by, enquiring if it was a holiday rental, eager to see inside. His house had always caused much interest in Samphire Bay. Jack had actually received a call from a national magazine that wanted to write an article on it. They were keen to tell the story of how it had been designed and built by him and his family. Whilst he'd been tempted, it was his dad who had put him off the idea. Although an article would have proved good publicity for both his and his son's businesses, Austin Knowles was a very shrewd man. He'd had reservations concerning the privacy element and, more importantly, security. Austin didn't want the world and its wife knowing about Jack's secluded beach house quietly tucked away in the cove. The locals admiring it was one thing, but it being publicly displayed for any devious opportunist to take advantage was quite another entirely.

Jack had agreed with his dad, which overall was a rarity. Both had strong views and opinions, often causing clashes, leading to notorious rows. The rest of the Knowles family simply learned to accept them. Jack's sister, Natalie, in particular was forced to when working with the pair of them. Being an interior designer, she had assisted Jack and together they had superbly furnished the beach house. But she had vowed never to get involved with a family project again. Playing mediator between her father and brother was pretty tiresome, never to be repeated, and she'd understood how difficult it must have been for their mum, forever being the referee between the two of them. No wonder their parents had been at pains to support Jack in building his house, they probably wanted peace and quiet in their own.

Above all, the Knowles family were extremely proud of Jack and what he'd achieved. And Jack was extremely proud of his family. Whilst he and his dad argued like cat and dog, he did respect him. He was well aware of how much money he'd saved him. Austin, being a highly skilled architect, would have cost Jack a fortune. Instead, he'd given his time, skill and advice totally free of charge – but it had cost Jack in other ways. He'd had to listen, keep quiet and take onboard everything his dad said. Well, almost. The Hot Tub Fiasco had proved a step too far. Austin had called it a 'costly, tacky and unnecessary indulgence', whereas for Jack it was a must, non-negotiable. In the end, Natalie had intervened to reach an agreement.

'Maybe allow a little luxury, as it's also going to be a family holiday home?' she'd suggested, appeasing the pair of them.

Once the fantastic house was built, all disagreements and quibbles were forgotten. The family had celebrated with a barbeque party on the beach. Natalie, her husband and their two boys were all bowled over with the cool, chalet-style holiday home. It had been worth it, she'd said as they played in the dunes, building sandcastles together. Still, she was in no hurry to do it all again.

Jack's mum was in awe of what they'd created. 'It's fabulous!' she'd gasped, seeing it for the first time. She hadn't followed the build's progress, choosing to stay well out of the way. Her view was to leave them to it, not wanting to get caught in any of the inevitable cross-fire between father and son. Looking at the finished house, she couldn't help but feel emotional, taking in the large glass windows, the smart wooden panelling and the wrap-around sundeck. Being inside a cove in the hillside gave lots of privacy and shelter, an ideal location. And the views! Such magnificent surrounding scenery. A huge sense of pride had swelled inside, for her husband as much as her son and daughter. It had been a real family accomplishment. It also touched her that Jack had insisted it was a family home, not just his. He wasn't territorial about the house at all, but wanted to share it. She only hoped her son would meet the perfect partner to live in it with. She'd glanced at Natalie and her happy little unit and so wanted the same for Jack. Once or twice she thought he'd met the right one, but, alas, they hadn't lasted. Maybe he was more like his dad than he realised, she wryly mused. It had taken a while for Austin to settle down too…

Ironically, Jack and his dad had toasted their build by clinking champagne glasses, whilst sitting in the bubbling hot tub outside on the decking.

'Here's to us, son, a job well done,' said Austin looking around admiring the place.

'Thanks, Dad,' replied Jack. Then he couldn't resist adding, 'Enjoying it in here?' He nodded towards the warm frothy water they sat in.

'Don't push your luck, Jack,' came the flat reply.

So, whilst Jack was very proud of his home, he was also conscious of who to invite inside. Obviously friends and family, but the frequent observers definitely not. Up until now. The latest inquisitive onlooker would be more than welcome to a personal guided tour. It was all in the timing. All he had to do was 'accidently' bump into her on the beach whilst on a run. He would stop, pretend to recognise her by chance, show her his hand and thank her again for stitching him up. Then he would casually ask her if she wanted a coffee at his nearby house, the stunning beach home she'd admired, thought Jack with a cunning smile. Oh yes, he could see it now. He loved it when a plan came together.

Chapter 12

Richard studied the letter before him once more, one elbow on the breakfast bar. A small part of him thought, *hoped*, that Tara had been bluffing. That she wasn't realistically about to go down this route. It was one thing her threatening him; she had done so in the past, but nothing had ever come of it. Now his eyes widened as he re-read just how far Tara was in fact prepared to go. She hadn't been joking when she'd told him of her solicitor friend's opinion of him. True to form, Claire had obviously persuaded Tara to fling everything possible at him.

He started to break into a sweat, again, as he took it all in. She wanted her pound of flesh all right, according to these figures. He gulped. For Richard knew that in the grand scheme of things, she was likely to get it. That bloody woman. Why now? It had been over a year since they'd parted (he hated referring to himself as 'leaving' his family; it pricked too hard on his conscience). In all that time, they had amiably made arrangements without any interference, especially from jumped-up Claire who he knew hated him.

He had to talk to Tara again, to reason with her. But even Richard knew that in order to do so he'd have to bring something to the table. Maybe up the maintenance a little? Or should he just offer her a lump sum, a one-off to shut her up once and for all? And *how* much would it take to stop the court proceedings? Exactly what would be the magic number Tara might settle for?

He continued to cast his eyes over the writing before him, stabbing him like a dagger to the heart. Tara wanted her share of the dental practice, claiming it was their joint finances that had funded the business initially. It had been. He couldn't argue with that. But surely the home, holidays and lifestyle the practice had provided her with had compensated? Richard refused to acknowledge that, actually, their home had been sold, the holidays ended and Tara's lifestyle had taken a drastic nosedive since he'd cleared off with his dental nurse. He ran a hand through his hair and gulped again. If his ex-wife got her way he'd be financially ruined, well, not exactly, he conceded, but certain measures would need to be made. His eyes then slid to Melissa who was entering the kitchen. Melissa didn't make measures. If anything, she exceeded them.

'Any post?' she asked, passing him and noticing he'd been reading something.

'Just junk mail.' He tried to sound as nonchalant as possible, when inside he was on meltdown. He quickly shoved the letter inside his trouser pocket. The last thing he needed was his new wife kicking up a fuss. Melissa did that all right. Oh yes, she definitely did. He winced at the thought of her getting wind of Tara taking her fair share – no, he quickly corrected himself, not her fair share, just what that cow Claire had instructed her to grab. The sooner he tried to resolve things with Tara the better.

'What have you got planned for today?' Melissa asked, putting the kettle on.

'Err... Nothing yet,' he answered, all the time plotting when it would be best to confront his ex-wife again.

'Good,' she answered. 'I thought we could go into town, look at prams.'

Richard's eyes closed in despair. That was another worry. A baby he absolutely hadn't planned. Another child. He remembered when Tara had announced her pregnancy years ago. How elated they'd both been. Somehow he just couldn't stump up the enthusiasm this time. Probably because he knew what was in store for him; sleepless nights followed by the joy of puberty. Now he was older and wiser – *older* being the operative word. He'd be one of the oldest dads at the school gate and the idea really didn't appeal to him. Richard was a very vain man. He'd loved having a young, attractive woman on his arm. He'd enjoyed the looks other men had slid his way. It gave him a buzz, bedding someone almost half his age. But instead of a youthful, fit wife who pandered to his every need, he now had a pregnant one who never stopped demanding. On top of this, it seemed he also had an ex-wife who was proving to be pretty demanding too. He slowly saw his future slipping between his fingers, unable to stop the flow of events. He didn't have control of his life any more. Or rather, he'd made choices and was about to suffer the consequences. He could imagine the looks other men were about to give him now. Pity. They'd be sympathetic, maybe even laughing, that he had had to start again at his age.

His thoughts got darker and darker the more he contemplated being a dad again. He remembered the early days with Calum and how difficult he'd been as a newborn. He'd suffered with dreadful colic which had meant endless sleepless nights. Richard also recalled how good Tara had been with him, constantly tending to their tiny baby who was crippled with pain. She had been a star, always keeping calm whilst administering Calum's medicine and gently comforting him. Whereas he'd been a complete wreck. He'd panicked, flustered, and was unable to function with lack of sleep. Tara had been the strong one, she had compensated for his lack. He did however make up for it by providing well for them. He'd worked hard at his surgery and made good money for his family. They'd been a great team. Once again he dully reflected on just what he'd given up, both the wife and the life. It was time to admit it to himself; he'd ballsed up – big time.

'Did you hear me, Richard?' Melissa's voice tinged with impatience.

That was another thing, he thought with sudden annoyance, the way she'd started talking to him, like she'd told him something twenty times before. He didn't answer her.

'Richard?' she snapped.

He looked up and stared into her face. Yes, he conceded, she was pretty enough with her big blue eyes and button nose, but her beauty he now realised didn't run deep. It was superficial, a veneer to hide what was inside. Melissa, he grasped, was only beautiful on the outside. And how had he come to this conclusion? Because she'd tricked him. Never had they ever discussed starting a family; in fact, she'd actually stated she didn't much care for motherhood. This had been one of the things that had attracted him. Richard had unwisely taken Melissa at her word. He genuinely believed they were on the same page. He stupidly thought that they would forever remain childless, always having that independent lifestyle he craved. He felt like weeping at the thought of saying goodbye to all the luxuries he enjoyed, which were about to be replaced with fatherhood, again. Only this time it would be worse. This time he didn't have a strong, capable wife to handle a crying newborn baby. He didn't have Tara. He had Melissa. Melissa, who had decided for him that they were starting a family. He'd had absolutely no say. He'd had absolutely *no idea* of his young wife's plans, which then made Richard gulp again. What else did she have planned? Could she be conspiring other things, like to divorce him in a few years' time? Would Melissa take him to the cleaners too?

'Are you listening to me?' she spat, moving towards him, her face butting up to his.

'Yes,' he answered wearily. What a fool he'd been.

He could hear Tara's voice in his head. There's no fool like an old fool, is there, Richard?

Chapter 13

Perry strolled down the coastal path, heading for the tidal road. He'd arranged to call on Emma and was looking forward to seeing her. Although he'd already visited the huge house on the peninsular since he'd got married, he'd gone with Bunty and whilst Felix had been there. Perry was anxious to see his daughter alone. He wanted to speak to her face to face, without anybody else present. For try as he might not to, he still worried about her. Yes, Emma was a fully grown woman who was more than capable of looking after herself, but he couldn't help how he felt.

Deep down, his biggest fear was the relationship she was in. Perry knew Emma was more than happy with Felix, and they did appear to be very suited, but there was a ten-year age gap between them. Bunty had laughed at him when he'd voiced his concern to her.

'Don't be silly, Perry! Ten years is nothing. There were almost twenty years between my parents,' she'd said.

Hmm, thought Perry, not comforted in the slightest. It had been sad that her mother had died so young though, leaving Bunty motherless at a very tender age. He expressly stopped his thoughts from wandering to her father. Perry did acknowledge that maybe Hamish Deville wouldn't have been so possessive and domineering over his daughter had he a wife to occupy him. Still, you couldn't rewrite history, he reflected, and really didn't want to taint his future happiness by mulling over it.

It wasn't just the age difference that concerned Perry. It was the fact Felix was a celebrity, well known, with people routinely recognising him on the street. He remembered his and Bunty's wedding, when their guests paid Felix more interest than them, the bride and groom! It irked Perry how Felix got all the attention, especially when Emma was by his side. *She* deserved to be star of the show, well, in Perry's eyes anyway.

He took a lungful of fresh sea air, enjoying the bracing walk. He'd driven along the coastal path many times, but being on foot gave him the time to appreciate his surroundings. Being a natural sailor, his eyes always gravitated to the water first. The sun shone vibrantly on the azure waves gently lapping against the shoreline. The cry of seagulls echoed in the distance. His gaze then slid to the rich golden horizon, casting shades of deep orange and yellow across the water. How magical it was.

Soon he reached the tidal road. Marching down the flat, sand-covered way, he saw that big, white art deco house that held many memories for both Bunty and him, though not all good. Perhaps he subconsciously judged Felix because he'd chosen to buy it? Emma loved it though, he admitted, which was the main thing.

Perry checked his watch, careful not to linger too long, being ever mindful of the incoming tide. He'd given himself plenty of time to get there and was making good pace. For a man of his age, he was in excellent shape. Perry had always been active, having sailed boats in his younger days and then living on a narrowboat in his later years. Life on a narrowboat had been pretty strenuous, but Perry had thrived on the exercise and exertion.

Reaching his destination, he walked up the stone steps and rang the bell. Emma soon answered it.

'Hi, Dad.' She hugged him hard and moved aside to let him in. Perry looked around the impressive, marbled hall.

'Felix here?' he asked casually, knowing he shouldn't be, but wanted it clarifying.

'No, he's in London on business, remember?' replied Emma.

'Oh yeah, that's right.' Perry nodded, relieved.

'Come to the kitchen. I've made us some lunch,' said Emma, directing him through to the stairs leading down there.

Once seated at the table eating sandwiches and drinking tea, Perry allowed himself to relax. He'd constantly felt a touch on edge in this house, despite trying desperately not to.

'So, what's Felix in London for?' asked Perry.

'The drama, of course. It's due to hit our screens mid-July. Felix can't wait, neither can I,' gushed Emma, making Perry smile. He loved her enthusiasm and zest. For Emma, this was a dream come true. Perry knew only too well of his daughter's aspirations.

'Will you be marking the occasion?' he grinned.

'Oh yes,' she trilled with gusto. 'We're throwing a party when the first episode airs.'

'Really?'

'Too right. You and Bunty are invited, obvs,' she told him.

'Great. Bunty will love it,' he replied, still smiling. He could just imagine his wife's reaction. She'd be at fever pitch.

'Felix says my voice will catapult me into fame,' she laughed. Perry stopped smiling.

'And is that what you want, Emma?' he quietly asked.

'What? To make it as a singer? You kidding?' she answered almost incredulously.

'I just don't want you to be overwhelmed, that's all.'

'Dad, you've always known how much I want to make it as a singer,' Emma replied, a touch exasperated.

'I know, I do, really...'

'But?' She eyed him carefully, sensing something was afoot.

'Are you ready, for what may lay ahead?'

'Such as?' She stared directly at him, arms crossed.

'The invasion of privacy. Look how Felix was hounded by the media,' replied Perry, trying to sound conciliatory. The last thing he needed was a fall-out with his daughter.

'You mean when he split up with his mad, psycho girlfriend? He was hardly to blame for that, Dad.' Emma was on the defensive now.

'No, of course not,' agreed Perry, wishing he'd never started this now. 'I just worry about you, that's all.'

Emma let out a sigh. 'Well, there's really no need. Felix bought this house because it offers privacy and seclusion, you know.'

Perry nodded. 'Yes, I know.'

'So, despite what you might think, we are protected here. There are security cameras all over this place.'

Perry refrained from referring to the incident of Felix's ex-girlfriend breaking in. What deterrent had the cameras been then? Deciding to change tack, he switched the subject.

'Who else will be coming to the party?' he asked.

Emma's face lit up immediately. 'Well, there's the cast, the production team and a few close friends, plus Felix's PA, Jennifer,' said Emma.

'Sounds good,' replied Perry, thinking how much his daughter had changed, and in such a short space of time. Gone were the days when she'd come home from working in the bank, sinking into the settee and asking what was for tea. Then again, he reflected, things had changed quite drastically for him also, and all for the better. So, why not for Emma too?

Chapter 14

Jack checked his watch yet again. Where was she? He so hoped to see Dr O'Hara again on the beach. It was Saturday morning, similar time to last week when she'd been jogging behind him. He decided to run down to the wooded area, where he suspected she must have come from.

Jack hadn't overdone his run so far, not wanting to appear too hot and sweaty. He'd also chosen to wear his most flattering tight hoodie and hugging tracksuit bottoms. To his elation, he could just about make out a figure coming through the pine trees. Squinting further, he saw a head of red hair. It was her! She was here! Nice and easy, Jack, he told himself, suddenly feeling a tad apprehensive, surprising even himself. Normally he wouldn't show any hesitation when approaching a woman, naturally having an air of confidence and charisma.

As coolly as he could, he ran up the beach towards her, planning ever so casually to stop for breath and wave up, hoping to instigate conversation. He took strong, firm strides as though demonstrating his powerful prowess. The figure in the distance was getting closer and closer. He took in her slim body in black leggings and a loose white T-shirt. She wore dark sunglasses blocking out the bright morning sunshine. She too was running at a steady pace.

As Jack got nearer he began to slow down, timing it with exact precision to meet her. Then, just as he approached her, he lost his footing and fell flat on the sand with a thud. Bloody hell, he cursed, of all the times to trip and fall. However, it did give him an advantage he quickly realised, when Tara hurried to his rescue.

'Are you OK?' she asked with concern, leaning over him. She'd taken off her sunglasses and Jack was gazing up at those stunning green eyes. He was fine actually, but never one to miss an opportunity, Jack decided to play it up a little to ensure her attention.

'I… think so.' He hesitated and winced when moving his left leg.

Immediately Tara knelt beside him. 'Here, let me see.' She felt his ankle then moved her hand over his calf muscle. 'Does it hurt?' she asked.

'Err…' Jack didn't want to admit it didn't in case she removed her hand and left him.

'Here, try standing,' said Tara. She held her hands out to help him up. Jack took them and stood with ease.

'I think I'm OK,' he said with a smile. Didn't she remember him, now his face was closer to hers? Obviously not. There was no trace of recognition from her. Then she looked at his hand, having felt the rough edge of his stitched scar.

Jack, seeing her glance at his wound, swiftly explained, 'You were the doctor in A&E who stitched my hand.'

'Oh yes, I remember.' She returned his smile, making Jack's insides melt. 'How's it been?'

'Hmm?' He was transfixed by her.

'The hand, how is it?' She tipped her head towards his stitches.

'Oh, fine, thanks. I'm back at work now.'

'Ah, I see. It's the warehouse by the quay in Lancaster you're renovating, isn't it?'

She remembered! 'Yes, that's right.' There was a slight pause.

'Well... If you're OK, I'll...' Tara was about to turn and start running again.

'Would you mind walking back home with me?' Jack hastily asked. 'Just in case I trip again?' He nodded towards his pretend injured leg.

'Of course. Where do you live?' asked Tara.

'Not far, just up there in the cove,' answered Jack rather smugly, anticipating her reaction.

'That beach house?' she replied in delight.

Jack nodded proudly. 'Yes. That's mine.'

'Oh, it's amazing! I noticed it the other day and was admiring it.'

I know, thought Jack with glee.

'Come on, I'll show you round if you want,' he grinned.

'Would you?' Her eyes widened with joy, giving Jack a warm glow inside.

'Yeah, of course. It's the least I can do. This is the second time you've come to my rescue,' he teased. How he loved it when a plan came together.

They chatted easily as they walked back up the beach to the cove. When they reached his house, Tara noticed how easily he ran up the wooden steps to the front door and smiled wryly to herself. His leg seemed to have mended very quickly, she noted.

Normally, she wouldn't have entertained the idea of entering a stranger's home alone, but it was plainly clear Jack genuinely wanted to show off his place. And why wouldn't he? Tara was totally in awe of it. Her eyes took in the hot tub on the decking outside and the seating area. It was absolutely ideal, a real sociable area. Her gaze then slid to Jack. Yes, he looked the outgoing kind. She imagined him throwing parties here, full of handsome men like him and glamorous girls, all laughing together. Tara doubted he'd be short of girlfriends and wondered if he had one. Could there be someone inside, waiting for him to return from his run? It was feasible, after all, that he was only being polite to her, returning a favour according to him.

As they entered the beach house, Tara was immediately taken by the panoramic views the huge windows gave. She whistled softly. Facing him, she was lost for words. Jack wallowed in satisfaction.

'It's Jack, by the way.' He offered a hand. He wasn't sure if she'd remembered his name from hospital, knowing she'd see a multitude of patients. 'Jack Knowles.'

'Tara O'Hara,' she replied with a firm handshake, then waited for the usual lip twitch her name often brought. And there it was, she thought drearily, seeing Jack's response.

'What a lovely rhymey name,' he said with a half-laugh.

'I chose to go back to my maiden name when I divorced.' She added in a flat tone, 'Tara O'Hara sounds better than Tara Totty.'

'Tara Totty?' spluttered Jack, totally unable to hide his amusement.

'Yeah,' she replied with a grim look.

'Dr Totty.'

'OK, don't rub it in.' Tara laughed, seeing the funny side. It was hard not to when looking at Jack. He obviously had a good sense of humour, which she liked, maybe because she wasn't used to it. Living with Richard had provided little fun and even less when separating from him. The only comedy she experienced was catching Calum in a good mood and sharing his teenage jokes. Tara suddenly realised how long it had been since she'd actually laughed with an adult.

'Oh, I don't know,' said Jack with a raised eyebrow, 'I rather think you suit the name Dr Totty.'

She rolled her eyes. If only she had a pound for every time she'd heard a connotation of that kind.

'Anyway,' Jack swiftly moved on, 'fancy a coffee?'

'Thanks.' She smiled, appreciating the change of subject.

Whilst Jack busied himself making the drinks, Tara continued her scrutiny of his home. The inside was every bit as impressive as the exterior, with its sleek modern kitchen and stylish furniture. He clearly has good taste, she concluded. She dearly longed to look upstairs but didn't dare ask. That really would appear intrusive.

'There you go.' Jack passed her a steaming mug.

'Thanks.'

He tipped his head towards the settee. 'Let's sit down.'

Once sat, Tara's eyes immediately drew to the glass gable end that overlooked the inside of the cove, giving a sense of being at one with the grey rock the house was built into.

'You must love living here,' she said in admiration.

'I do. I never take it for granted. So much work went into designing and building it.'

'I bet.'

'My dad, sister and I worked on it,' he announced proudly.

'Really?' Tara asked in surprise.

'Yeah, my dad's an architect and Natalie, my sister, is an interior designer.'

'That figures.' She nodded. Then, a penny suddenly dropped. Jack's surname was Knowles... and his dad was an architect.

Seeing her expression, Jack frowned. What was she thinking?

'It was a real family project,' he continued, eyeing her carefully.

'Is your family connected to Knowles & Carter Architects?' she asked.

'Yes, that's my dad's business,' he replied in surprise. 'Do you know it?'

'Oh, only from a friend, that's all. I think your dad designed an extension of hers.' And that's not all, she thought tartly. So, Jack was Austin Knowles' son... Well, well.

Chapter 15

Jack couldn't stop talking about his encounter with Dr O'Hara, or as he now knew her, Tara. He'd gone into work the following day full of optimism. However, there was one *slight* reservation. It had been clear to Jack that the mention of his dad's company, if not his name, had caused a reaction in Tara. He wasn't fully convinced of her explanation either. To him it sounded a touch lame. A horrid, dull feeling washed over him when contemplating it. Surely she didn't have any 'connection' to him? He hated to admit it, but his father did have form, as much as his poor mother – and the rest of the family – hated to admit it. But there it was, forever hovering in the background like a bad smell.

Austin Knowles had had an affair. If Jack was being completely honest with himself, he suspected the affair that very nearly split his parents up hadn't been the only one. It was certainly the only one he and his sister had known about, but, looking back over his childhood with adult eyes, Jack was persuaded his dad had always played away. Incidences flashed through his mind; mum in tears, late at night, waiting for her husband to return home; the stilted, silent breakfasts charged with tension; the forced, false bravado she often displayed – all this had begun to make sense to Jack and his sister now. He also, as an adult, saw how attractive his dad was to women. Basically, he was an older version of himself. Not only did people compare them in personality, but looks too. Jack knew exactly how he was going to age, just by looking at his dad. But Jack was adamant that he wasn't going to end up like his dad and vowed to himself he'd always be faithful and never cheat on his wife.

When he'd raised the matter with Natalie, she'd been evasive, not wanting to discuss their father's indiscretions too much. And anyway, it was all in the past, she'd said. Well, almost. Jack totally understood, he didn't' want to think badly of his dad either, and besides, ever since the affair they all knew about a couple of years ago, his parents seemed to have been happy together.

Even so, he couldn't forget the look on Tara's face when she realised his dad was Austin Knowles. Should he have questioned her further? No, he reasoned, it might have appeared a little odd. Instead he decided to accept her explanation. Given time, the right moment may rear its head when he could probe deeper. For now though, Jack was just pleased he'd finally made contact and that it had gone so well.

Before Tara had left, he'd asked her out for a drink, which she'd been pleased to accept.

'I'll introduce you to our local,' he'd suggested.

'Ah yes, The Smugglers. I'd like that,' Tara replied with a smile.

So, with a hot date on the horizon, Jack had a spring in his step as he entered the warehouse to find Robin studying the plans.

'Hi, Rob,' he said, breezing in.

Robin looked up, surprised. 'You seem in a good mood.' He smirked, knowing what was to follow. He wasn't wrong.

'Oh, I am. The time has come,' he announced with a wide beam on his face.

Robin laughed. 'Don't tell me. You've made contact with Dr O'Hara?'

'It's Tara now, actually,' replied Jack rather smugly.

'Of course it is,' said Robin with a grin, pleased for his friend, but not at all shocked. Jack then filled him in, omitting the detail about his dad. 'So, you're meeting her again then?' asked Robin with a sly smile.

'Yep, taking her to The Smugglers,' answered Jack with a wink. 'Anyway, what were you looking at?' He tipped his head towards the sheet of paper Robin held.

'The adjoining walls,' replied Robin.

'Right, which ones are coming down?' said Jack, studying the detailed plans. 'These two?' He pointed to the area that was going to comprise of the first two apartments to be renovated.

'I think so,' agreed Robin. 'Then we can concentrate on the reconfiguration of flats one and two.'

'Good.' Jack rubbed his hands together, eager to get on. He loved this stage in the process, when the building was about to become an empty shell, ready for them to make an impact and put their stamp on it. Robin rolled up the sheet.

'OK, let's get the sledgehammers,' said Jack. He loved knocking down walls too. It gave him a real sense of satisfaction, plus it was good exercise and let off any built-up tension.

Later that day, after he and Robin had bashed down the two walls and cleared all the debris away, Jack drove home knackered and in dire need of a hot, relaxing bath. Striding up the wooden steps, his eyes cast over the hot tub on the decking. Oh, sod it, he thought, he was going in there tonight. After switching it on and letting it heat up while he had a quick shower, Jack changed into his swimming trunks and eased himself into the soothing, simmering water.

'Ah,' he sighed, eyes closed, relishing the sensation. He had a bottle of beer propped on the side and reached out for it. The cool liquid refreshed him. He looked up at the dark sky spotted with stars. 'This is the life,' he told himself with contentment. The only thing missing was Tara.

Once again, his thoughts turned to yesterday and how well they'd got on. She was easy to talk to, no empty silences or awkwardness… apart from the mention of his dad. Jack begrudged that his dad had made him feel this way. In reality, Jack resented his dad full stop. Yes, he *was* a good father in many ways. He'd helped him tremendously in the past, no question. But what Jack resented was the *husband* his dad had made. His mother was a saint for tolerating him. Jack hated it when she joked about him being like his dad.

'Like father, like son,' she'd often say, but to Jack this simply wasn't true. OK, so he'd had a reputation for being 'Jack the Lad', but that was ages ago, when he'd been younger. He liked to think he'd outgrown that. Now, in his early thirties, Jack's attitude had changed, of course it had. It was frustrating sometimes, the way people treated him, like Rob for instance. He knew his best friend hadn't taken him seriously about Tara. But why? Because they'd been like brothers since the age of seventeen and he'd known him in his heyday, Jack analysed. Even so, he didn't want Robin to assume Tara was going to be just another fling. Well, she wasn't going to be, was she? Plus, Tara was a mum, there was a son to consider, which Jack took very seriously. A cold chill ran up his spine at the thought of ending up like his dad. No, he told himself sternly, he wouldn't. He'd seen the damage caused to his mum. He definitely was not going to be like his dad. All he needed was the love of a good woman, that's all, and up until now he hadn't met the right one.

He tried to rationalise his innate attraction towards Tara. Was it because she was a doctor? Did he subconsciously trust and feel secure in some way? She was certainly goodlooking, that's for sure, clearly looked after herself, was intelligent and showed a caring side. A perfect combination in Jack's eyes.

Jack took another gulp of beer and leaned his head back against the side of the hot tub. With his eyes closed, he tried to relax and get in the zone. Allowing the soft bubbles to flow over him, he breathed in deeply, then out slowly, listening to the sound of the shore. How blissfully peaceful it was out here, enveloped in the cove. And, he reminded himself, none of this would have happened without his dad. He also had a lot to thank his father for too.

Chapter 16

'So, Jack's smitten, is he?' Jasmine grinned as she placed dinner on the table. Robin had been discussing his day at work and how upbeat Jack was.

Whilst pleased his best mate had met up with Tara, he still couldn't help but be amused by the whole thing. It was typical of Jack to be so keen at the start of a relationship. Robin had seen it many times before, where his friend went all in, guns blazing, only to lose interest further down the line. It was as if Jack revelled in the chase more than anything. Robin had lost count of the number of women that Jack had sworn was 'the one', only to see the relationship fail for one reason or another.

'Well, for now anyway,' replied Robin.

'What do you mean?' asked Jasmine with a frown.

'Until the novelty wears off I guess.'

'How do you know it will?' Jasmine sounded a touch surprised. 'Maybe Jack's ready to settle.'

Robin considered her words. Perhaps Jack *was* ready to settle down. He reflected on his friend's recent behaviour, noticing a change in him. Whereas Jack was normally full of fun and spirit, he'd seemed subdued of late. He was, and always had been, the life and soul of every party, but, Robin conceded, he'd known Jack since he was seventeen. Could Jasmine be right? Maybe he was tired of drifting in and out of relationships and wanted that special person in his life. After all, they were the same age and look at him. He was more than happy with Jasmine and looking forward to parenthood. Why shouldn't Jack want the same?

'You're right. Perhaps Dr O'Hara could be the one to finally tame Jack,' said Robin thoughtfully.

'You never know,' replied Jasmine. Then added, 'He could bring her to Emma and Felix's party?'

Robin frowned.

'The party to celebrate Felix's drama being aired?' reminded Jasmine.

'Oh, yeah. Actually, that's a good idea, it'd be a great chance for us all to meet her.'

'And it'll be so fascinating, being inside that lovely big house, among all the cast of *Lady Scarlett Investigates*.' Jasmine was looking forward to the do immensely. The invites had only just arrived that morning and she assumed Jack would have received one too, knowing from Bunty that Emma intended to invite him. Out of Samphire Bay, the only villagers invited to attend the party were Bunty and Perry, Jasmine and Robin, Jack and a plus one.

Jasmine got up from the table and reached for the invite on the kitchen worktop.

'Here, look.' She handed the card to Robin.

'Very classy,' he remarked, taking in the black background with silver art deco writing. Lady Scarlett appeared in the centre, dressed in a 1920s flapper dress, holding up a cocktail glass with a cheeky wink.

Come to the launch of Lady Scarlett Investigates.

Saturday, 19 July at 2 p.m.

Charades, The Tidal Road, Samphire Bay.

'Charades?' said Robin. 'Since when has Bunty's old house been called Charades?' He sniggered.

'Apparently Felix gave it that name for the drama and decided to keep it. I rather like it,' replied Jasmine. Then her face suddenly contorted in pain, but quickly recovered.

'Are you all right?' Robin checked.

'Yes, just a twinge. They're on the move again,' Jasmine answered, rubbing her swollen belly.

'Sure?' he persisted.

'Yeah, honestly, I'm fine,' she promised, smiling.

Perry was reading his invitation too whilst smiling to himself. Knowing full well how Bunty was going to react, he left it on the mantelpiece in view for her to see it. It didn't take long for Bunty to notice.

'Oh, look!' she exclaimed, quickly picking it up to read, then couldn't help but giggle at the house name. 'Fancy my childhood home having such a playful name,' she laughed.

'Suits it though, doesn't it?' replied Perry. Personally, he found the name far more palatable than calling it 'the big white house on the peninsula', as it was often referred to.

'Yes, I suppose it does,' answered Bunty, already excited to attend the party. 'It's going to be such fun,' she trilled, imagining the house alive with music and dance, not to mention watching the opening episode of the *Lady Scarlett Investigates* drama. It would be so intriguing to see her former house as the home of the superstar sleuth. Amazing really, considering how events had turned out.

Who would have thought of Felix Paschal buying the place and actually directing a TV series there? It beggared belief. She wondered what her family would have made of it all. Bunty suspected her mother would have been delighted, having a real fondness for the art deco period. She no doubt would have enjoyed every minute. As for Daddy... Well, she knew damn well he'd have hated the very idea. Still, he wasn't here now, was he? And Bunty had no intention of letting him nor his memory ruin anything again for her.

'It'll be wonderful hearing Emma sing,' sighed Perry with pride.

'Absolutely,' agreed Bunty, again considering the turn of events. If she hadn't decided to sell her house, there wouldn't have been an open house day and no piano in the hall. For it had been the estate agent's idea to decorate the huge, marbled entrance with a grand piano. Emma had sung and played the instrument, looking every bit the part. Felix Paschal had clearly been taken with both her and the house, declaring he'd buy the place after hearing her sing, providing the piano was part of the sale. And the rest was history. Bunty smiled affectionately. She was so glad her childhood home was in such good hands – and that she still had connections to it.

—

Jack, on reading his invite, raised an eyebrow. *Hmm, very interesting*, he thought, seeing it as an ideal opportunity to involve Tara. Who wouldn't want to meet the rich and famous? He could picture it now; him, looking suave and sophisticated, introducing her to his friends, well, a couple of them anyway, milling around the impressive rooms, rubbing shoulders with the stars, sipping champagne… Oh yes, she couldn't help but be impressed. Yes, he'd invite her at their date at The Smugglers.

His thoughts then turned to tomorrow night, when he was meeting Tara. They had exchanged mobile numbers the day she'd been at his house, after he'd asked her out. Tara had explained that being a single parent could often involve a change of plan. 'It should be fine, but just in case,' she'd told him. 'Calum is due to be at his dad's that evening.'

Jack checked his phone again, making sure there were no messages and all was on track. Good, there wasn't one. Everything was still on.

For once, Jack had decided in advance on what to wear for his date. Usually, he'd just open his wardrobe and pull out the first thing to hand. In fact, he'd even bought a new outfit. The pale grey shirt highlighted his eyes perfectly.

The invite to the party had come at just the right time. It would make great conversation, thought Jack. Actually watching the first episode of the TV drama would be exciting too, especially amongst all the cast. Yeah, it was definitely going to be a good night, and for once, he wouldn't feel like a gooseberry with Robin and Jasmine, he'd have a partner too.

Chapter 17

Tara had just dropped Calum off at his dad's. She waved to her son, refusing to even look at Richard who had answered the door. He'd only have a 'look' to give her, whether it be a needy puppy-eyed one or a tight stare of contempt, depending on his mood. Quite frankly, she was past caring how Richard felt. At one time she'd try to pacify his moods, but it was no longer any of her concern, thankfully.

Driving back home alone, Tara reflected on just how much she had pandered to her ex-husband, forever bending over backwards to keep him happy. And for what? Richard had never appreciated her, always taking his wife for granted. Memories flooded her mind; all the boozy nights out he'd had with his friends, whilst her social life had been pretty non-existent since having Calum. Then there were the weekend aways he'd often go on, whether it be for the rugby, stag dos or any other excuse he'd come up with. Richard thought nothing of leaving her at home with their son, whilst he cleared off to do his own thing.

It was because of this independent lifestyle Richard had carved out for himself that had enabled him to have an affair so easily. Tara had become used to him not being around all the time. She had never suspected a thing. Only once, when she'd seen a bank statement containing a hotel payment. She had queried it with him, but he'd given an excuse that there was no room available at the digs his mates had booked, so he'd had to go to a separate hotel. Looking back, Tara cursed herself for not pursuing it further. Had she done so, she'd have soon realised the five-star country hotel was nowhere near the supposed rugby match. She'd have also realised that there hadn't even been a rugby match. That weekend had been the first of many nights spent with Melissa. Only after the divorce did Tara piece it all together and hated herself for being so trusting with him. But, she conceded, shouldn't she have been able to trust her own husband? Apparently not.

Anger still flared inside her, especially when she considered how Richard had dealt with their separation, in particular the financial matters. When it came to money, he was definitely astute. Not only was he clever, but very manipulative. Tara could see this now, looking objectively from the periphery, as opposed to being stuck in the thick of it. Now that the dust had settled, she could see far more clearly. She understood Claire's frustration at the terms she'd initially agreed on. It was almost laughable, had it not been so sad. The fact she'd allowed her ex-husband to grind her down and relent so much to him was indeed sad.

Then Tara took a deep breath and gripped the steering wheel. She'd got through it. She'd finally seen sense and was doing something about it, being proactive and 'getting back control of her life,' as Claire had said. The court hearing date was looming and obviously affecting Richard. She could tell by the way he was acting and from the feedback Calum was giving her. Apparently all was not well in his household. Calum had noted an atmosphere and overheard a few heated discussions. This in itself gave Tara a degree of satisfaction. Thinking of brighter things, she contemplated her date tonight with Jack. She so wanted a change of scene, good company and a few drinks. It had felt like an age since she'd let her hair down and had some fun.

A few hours later, Tara stood in front of the mirror scrutinising her reflection. Not bad, she thought. Deciding on smart but casual, she wore slim-fitting jeans and a wraparound tunic with a brown, orange and cream pattern, which complimented her hair and complexion nicely. She even painted her nails, something she hadn't done in years. Then again, it had been a while since she'd gone on a date. All of a sudden, Tara felt a pang of anxiety. She stared at her reflection in the mirror. 'You can do this,' she told herself.

They'd arranged to meet in The Smugglers. It wasn't a long walk from where she lived and she preferred to go on foot, rather than be picked up by Jack. Striding out of Augusta House and onto the tidal road leading to the pub, Tara breathed in the fresh, salty sea air. Spring had fully edged its way into Samphire Bay and a pleasant breeze whispered through the sea-grass, gently swaying in the late evening sunshine. She took a right turn, down towards the village. How quaint this place was, thought Tara, taking in a row of pretty white cottages with colourful front lawns divided by picket fences, a medieval church and a village hall. There was a cobbled square containing a large stone cross. The Smugglers was a sandstone building with mullion windows, an ancient oak door and pink-and-white geraniums stood in terracotta pots by the entrance.

Heads turned as Tara walked into the busy pub. It wasn't often the locals witnessed a stunning redhead pass by them with such cool composure. Jack saw her immediately and waved up. Her face broke into a smile at noticing him and she made her way to his table. Jack received a few sly glances, which he ignored.

'Hi.' He stood up to greet her and smiled.

Tara grinned back. 'Hi.'

'What are you drinking?'

'A white wine would be lovely, thanks,' replied Tara, resisting the urge to say 'a large one'.

Jack soon came back carrying a glass of wine and another pint for himself. One or two of the men at the bar had uttered a few comments to him, which he'd nonchalantly batted away. It was inevitable Tara would cause a stir, being new blood to the pub, and looking so attractive too. Jack felt proud to be with her.

'There you go.' He placed the drinks down and sat opposite her.

'Thanks,' said Tara and took a mouthful. She closed her eyes, savouring the cool, zesty flavour.

Jack gazed at her and laughed. 'You look like you needed that.'

Tara blew out a gusty sigh. 'I did.'

'Yeah, it must be very stressful working in A&E.'

'That's the easy part,' she said with a wry grin, instantly wishing she hadn't.

'Sorry?' asked Jack confused.

'Oh, nothing... just...' Hell, *why* had she started this line of conversation? She took another gulp of wine. 'It's been a pretty demanding year, what with a divorce and moving.'

'I see. They are two of the main causes of stress in life,' Jack said sympathetically.

'Tell me about it,' replied Tara dryly.

'You can tell me about it,' answered Jack softly.

Tara looked into his eyes, which held real compassion. She was tempted, so tempted to simply offload and spill all the angst out. But no, not now. This wasn't the time or place for that discussion. Tonight was about having fun and getting to know each other, not the serious, depressing stuff.

'Maybe, but not now,' she said, then swiftly changed the subject. 'How's the renovation going?'

Jack's face immediately lit up as he outlined the plans for the warehouse. Tara was impressed by the enthusiasm he showed for his work. All the time she couldn't help but notice the attention he seemed to be receiving, whether it was knowing smirks from the locals or admiring glances from the women nearby. One or two called out to him and he nodded back with a smile. Obviously well-known and popular, thought Tara. After he finished telling her about his project, Jack asked about Calum.

'What does your son think of Samphire Bay?'

'Well, he loves the apartment, particularly his bedroom balcony,' she answered, 'but I think he's still getting used to new surroundings.'

'Sure.' Jack nodded, then added, 'But it's a fantastic place to grow up. Me and Robin loved it here; parties on the beach, skinny dipping in a moonlit sea, we had a ball,' he chuckled.

Tara laughed, picturing him and Robin living it up together in such a fabulous location. She so wanted the same for Calum.

'And it's now home to none other than Felix Paschal,' continued Jack.

'Yeah, I heard he bought that house on the peninsula,' said Tara, then watched him pull something out of his pocket.

'It's an invite,' Jack told her, passing it over. He examined those gorgeous green eyes of hers dart across the card, reading all the details. She looked up at him. 'Would you like to come?' he asked, a touch self-satisfying.

'Seriously? How come you've got an invite?' said Tara, amazed.

Jack explained his connection to Bunty and Emma, all the while Tara sat and listened in awe. She glanced again at the date and tried to calculate if she'd be working, then paused. She'd take annual leave if need be. There was no way she was missing this.

'Of course. I'd love to come!' Tara beamed.

Not bad for a first date, thought Jack smugly. Not bad at all.

Chapter 18

The following day Tara couldn't stop looking at the invite Jack had given her. He'd told her to keep it, seeing how delighted she'd been to receive an invitation. She put it on the kitchen worktop and was just admiring it again. The launch party was clearly set to be a glamorous affair, judging by the company expected there and the location. Like many, Tara had stood on the bay, looking out to the peninsula at the huge art deco house stood proudly there. It cut quite an imposing structure, all alone apart from the clifftops and roaring sea beneath it.

Very dramatic, thought Tara, and how apt to be hosting the first episode of a 1920s murder mystery drama. It filled Tara with a sense of thrill, something she hadn't experienced in a very long time.

It hadn't always been this way, reflected Tara. She had felt a thrill when first meeting Richard, that first flush of romance when getting to know someone. Richard had wowed her then, back in the day. Being a little older than her, she'd felt almost protected by him. He'd been in the last year of his medical degree as she was just starting. He'd shown her the ropes around the campus and assisted enormously with her studies. He'd made her life at university practically stress-free, forever cooking meals, helping her revise and encouraging her. Richard had been her rock, a sturdy, reliable man who could be depended on. He was also easy on the eye. His large frame was toned by all the rugby he played, which hadn't gone unnoticed by Tara's roommates.

Yes, she'd been envied by her friends at university and at home when bringing Richard back to meet her mum and dad. They'd liked him too, everybody had. Apart from Claire. She'd never taken to him. Tara's parents had particularly warmed to him when seeing how good he was with their daughter once she got pregnant. It hadn't been planned, far from it. Being twenty years old with child at university was definitely not in the script. This was where Richard really surpassed himself, insisting he take care of her and do practically everything possible for Tara. Apart from attending lectures, he couldn't have done more. By this time he'd completed his studies and had started working in a dental practice. He rented a house near to the university and moved Tara in. They'd been happy together, a real team. Over the years, as Tara had also finished her studies, they'd gone from strength to strength, each supporting the other in their careers.

Once again Tara reminisced the day they had bought their beautiful Georgian house, how proud they'd been to have such a stunning home. This was then followed with the memory of Richard setting up his own dental practice, marking the downfall of their marriage. That's when it all went wrong; because with the new business, came Melissa.

Looking back, Tara often wondered, if Richard hadn't bought his own practice, would he have remained faithful? Or would it simply have been a matter of time before his eyes wandered? Was there always going to be a Melissa waiting in the wings, ready to destroy her family? She knew Richard was vain, loving any form of attention, maybe it was inevitable, always on the cards?

Anyway, she inhaled deeply, it was all in the past. What was done was done. There was no turning back now. As if on cue, the intercom buzzed, it was Calum returning. Pressing the entry button, she was later surprised to hear voices in the corridor. Calum used his key to open the door and behind him followed Richard. Tara frowned, not expecting to see him. Calum looked at her somewhat apologetically and rolled his eyes, knowing his dad's presence wouldn't be wanted here.

'I parked on the roadside,' explained Richard. Tara stared at him, knowing full well he'd done that to avoid alerting her. Had he parked in the Augusta House car park, she'd have had to let him in – or not, which is why he chose to surprise her and walk in with Calum.

As usual Calum went straight to his room, he sensed an argument brewing and wanted out of the way.

Tara folded her arms and raised an eyebrow. 'Well?' she asked cooly.

'I… err… thought we might have a chat,' answered Richard hesitantly.

Tara sighed. Here we go again, she thought dully. He was relentless. She turned to make herself a drink.

'Please, hear me out,' he whined, following her to the kitchenette.

'Look, Richard, there's really nothing left to say,' she replied witheringly.

'But…' His eyes darted to the invite on the countertop. Tara noticed and objected to him blatantly picking it up to read.

'Do you mind? Put that back,' she ordered. She watched his face twist with resentment.

'What's this?' he snapped, waving the card in the air.

The cheek of the man! Tara whipped it from his hand.

'No concern of yours,' she spat back.

'Rubbing shoulders with the rich and famous?' he snorted. 'How did you bag that?' His tone was cruel and mocking. Tara didn't gratify him with an answer, just stared him coldly in the face. 'So, who are you going there with?' he asked, tipping his chin up arrogantly.

'Mind your own business,' she replied flatly. This infuriated him even more.

'*Who*, Tara?' he demanded.

'Get out!' she shouted, making him flinch.

'Mum?' Calum came into the kitchen looking uneasy.

'It's OK, love. Dad was just leaving.' Tara tried to sound as reassuring as possible. Calum looked from one parent to the other. Richard coughed.

'Yes... I'll be on my way now, son.'

Tara gave him an evil look and marched to the door. Opening it, she stood waiting for him to move.

'Right, see you soon, Calum.' He turned, but Calum had disappeared back into his room.

'Out,' Tara repeated, seething with anger. Richard reluctantly made his way to the door, shoulders drooped, defeated. He paused, as if to try speaking to her one last time, but she turned away. Once he passed into the corridor Tara slammed the door shut and bolted it. That was the very last time he'd step foot in here. From now on she'd have to prep Calum into entering Augusta House alone, or at least warn her if his dad intended to visit. Poor Calum, she closed her eyes and fought the urge to cry. Tapping on his bedroom door, she gently called out to him. 'Calum, can I come in?'

'Yeah.'

Entering, she saw the balcony doors open and him sat on the bistro chairs out there. He removed his legs for her to sit down opposite him.

'I'm sorry about that,' she said quietly.

'It's not your fault,' he replied, then looked out to the view of the bay. 'It's Dad's fault. It's all Dad's fault.' His voice was hushed and low, on the verge of tears. This cut Tara up. She *hated* what Richard was doing to their son. Then Calum turned to face her. 'What was all that about anyway?'

'I'll show you.' Tara got up to fetch the invitation. On returning, she passed it to Calum to read. His solemn face slowly broke into a grin.

'Cool,' he said, giving it back to her. Then asked, 'Who are you going with?'

Tara told him all about Jack, how she met him, where he lived and his connection to Emma and Felix Paschal.

He whistled. 'Double cool.'

Chapter 19

Jack was on cloud nine. Pleased with how well his date had gone, he felt buoyed up and decided to visit his parents. He knew how Samphire Bay operated and assumed it highly likely that they would have already been told about their son and the attractive newcomer meeting in The Smugglers.

True to form, as he entered their kitchen he was greeted with a knowing grin from his mum.

'Hi, Mum,' said Jack, plonking himself down by the table.

'Hiya, love, fancy a brew?'

'Thanks. Where's Dad?'

'At Natalie's. He should be home soon,' she replied whilst putting the kettle on. Then, unable to resist, she turned and asked, 'So, who's the redhead you were seen with in The Smugglers?'

Typical, thought Jack. It had taken all of one minute for the interrogation to start.

'Sorry?' He decided to act dumb.

'Don't give me that, Jack!' His mum chuckled, knowing full well what he was doing. She joined him at the table with two cups and sat down. 'You were seen at The Smugglers with a pretty red-haired lady.' Jack frowned, continuing to fake confusion. 'New to Samphire Bay, I believe she's bought Robin's apartment?'

She was well informed, noted Jack, wondering what else she knew about Tara.

'Yes, she does live in Robin's old apartment,' admitted Jack. 'Out of interest, who told you that?' he asked.

'Ned told us this morning at church.'

Ned, of course, the pub landlord. Nothing got past him – and nothing stayed with him either.

'So come on then, spill the beans.'

'Her name's Tara and I met her in hospital, where she's a doctor in A&E. She's the doctor who stitched up my hand.' He lifted it up to show his mum her handywork.

'Really?' His mum sounded keen to know more.

'Yes. Total coincidence that she bought Robin's place and then I bumped into her jogging on the beach.'

'Aw, that's nice.' She smiled, eyes twinkling. Could this be the one? She certainly hoped so. It was about time her son settled down.

Jack grinned wryly to himself, knowing precisely what was going through her mind.

'Tara, that's a nice name too,' she continued, looking wistfully into space.

Jack openly laughed, suspecting she was now imagining wedding bells and him in a dark morning suit alongside a red-haired bride.

'What?' she asked, almost indignantly.

'You. You're so transparent, Mum,' teased Jack.

'What do you mean?' It was her turn now to faux confusion.

'You were marrying me off with her, weren't you?' he asked dryly.

'Well...' They were interrupted by Jack's dad returning home.

'Oh, hi, Jack. Didn't expect to see you here,' he called, entering the kitchen. 'Thought you might be busy.' He gave a cheeky wink, making Jack roll his eyes.

'What, you meant with the hot redhead?' he replied with sarcasm.

His dad laughed in response. 'Something like that. Who is she then?' He came to sit with them at the table.

'She's a doctor, works in A&E,' gushed his mum.

His dad arched an eyebrow. 'I see.'

'And she's called Tara,' she continued.

Jack studied his father's face, keen to see his reaction. He hadn't forgotten how Tara had reacted to knowing his dad's name. Up to now he hadn't seen anything untoward. He decided to test the water further.

'Tara O'Hara. Dr Tara O'Hara,' he stated, all the time scrutinising his dad. And there it was: a slight flicker of recognition, very small, but definitely there. There was a momentary lull. 'Have you heard of her, Dad?' asked Jack, trying to sound as casual as possible, when inside he intrinsically knew this was a big deal. He could feel it in his bones.

'Me? No, why should I?' replied his dad, sounding very convincing. Too convincing, in Jack's opinion, remembering how good his dad was at covering up the truth, and his tracks. His eyes slid over to his mum, who seemed oblivious to any awkwardness. Perhaps he was imagining it? The phone rang, disrupting his thoughts as his mum dashed off to answer it.

Once alone, Jack decided to push further.

'Tara has heard of you,' he said conversationally.

'How?' His dad's voice held a slight edge to it.

'I think you've done some work for her friend... an extension or something...?' Jack's gaze never left his dad's face. He noticed his eyelid twitch, a sure tell-tale sign, as it was a nervous tick his dad had whenever he was suffering with stress. A part of Jack loathed what he was doing, testing his own father, but another part of him needed to know the truth. What exactly was the connection between Tara and his dad? And would it be enough to put him off? He gulped, hating being in this predicament. Was he about to open a can of worms? Uncover something that deep down he'd really rather not know?

'Well, I could have done, that's possible. In fact probable,' reasoned his dad.

He was right, conceded Jack. Knowles & Carter Architects were a well-known, reputable firm. It wouldn't be unusual for someone in the area to have used them. Was he letting his imagination run away with him? Looking for trouble that simply didn't exist?

'You know, Jack, all me and your mum want is for you to be happy,' said his dad, looking him in the eye.

'Yeah, I know,' frowned Jack, wondering why his dad should suddenly make such a statement.

'Then I suggest you just relax and enjoy getting to know Tara. Let nature take its course.'

A switch flicked inside Jack. Something his dad was an expert at doing. Was he intimating that his relationship with Tara was destined to end, like all the others? Was the 'let nature take its course' comment a dig, meaning all his relationships naturally ended, never fully blossoming into fruitful ones? A flare of anger shot through him as he flashed a glare of contempt towards his father, who was still managing to look perfectly at ease, apart from that twitching eyelid. That's what was giving him away, and Jack knew it.

'You're right, Dad. I *do* intend to get to know Tara,' Jack replied whilst staring his dad full in the face.

'Good.' His dad nodded.

'Yeah, I want to be open and honest, hopefully build a decent relationship,' he continued.

'Exactly,' replied his dad with a tight smile.

'Because honesty's the best policy. Isn't that right, Dad?'

Their eyes met. Suddenly Jack's mum came back into the kitchen.

'That was Natalie. You've left your phone there, Austin.'

'Bloody hell,' he cursed himself.

'I can fetch it,' said Jack. 'I was going to call round there anyway.'

'Would you mind?' replied his mum. 'That would be helpful, wouldn't it?' She looked towards her husband.

'Sure, if that's OK with you, Jack?'

'Fine. No trouble.'

Truth be told, Jack wanted to speak to his sister. All this business with his father was unsettling him. That's if there *was* anything actually going on, and not just his overactive mind playing tricks. He loved Natalie, she grounded him, always put things in perspective.

Leaving his parents' house, with a promise to return soon with the forgotten phone, Jack's mood had sadly shifted somewhat.

It took Jack just under an hour to reach Natalie's house, since she lived on the outskirts of Buckshaw village.

'Hey, Jack!' she called when she saw him walk down the driveway. She was on the front lawn, gardening.

'Hi, I've come to collect Dad's phone,' he said, rolling his eyes.

'Oh, right, he sent you, did he?' Natalie laughed. 'Come on, let's have a cuppa. The kids are out with their dad,' she said, taking off her gardening gloves.

Jack was pleased to have caught his sister alone. They were soon sat in the conservatory sipping tea, and Natalie nodded towards the glass coffee table where the forgotten mobile phone was.

'Put that in your pocket, before you forget to take it,' she told him.

Jack slid the phone into his inside jacket pocket. It felt hard against his ribcage. Could it contain any vital evidence? Any incriminating text messages? Or secret contacts? Was he going to search his dad's phone once alone? Yes, of course he was. He felt justified, his rationale being that his father surely wouldn't have anything to hide, or, if he did, then he deserved to be found out.

'What's the matter, Jack?' Natalie frowned, wondering why her brother looked so pensive.

He let out a sigh. 'Natalie, I've met someone,' he began to explain.

'Who?' she asked excitedly, sitting forward, all ears.

'She's called Tara and I met her in hospital. She's the doctor who stitched up my hand.'

'Really?'

'Yeah. Tara's great...'

'But?' replied Natalie a touch warily.

Jack gave another deep sigh. 'She knows Dad, or at least of him.'

There was a slight pause.

'How?' she asked quietly. Jack could tell by the tone of her voice that her line of thought was pretty much on the same wavelength as his.

'Tara said he did some work for her friend...'

'Well then, that's totally feasible,' reasoned Natalie.

'No, I'm sure there's more to it. Just the way her face and body language changed when learning who my dad was. And also with Dad when I asked him about Tara. He went all cagey.'

'Cagey?'

'Yeah, well, on the surface he appeared OK, but that nervous twitch he has appeared.'

'Oh,' she flatly replied, knowing exactly what her brother was talking about. She sat back in silence.

'I don't really know what to do,' continued Jack. 'Just when I've met someone special, this happens.'

'You could just ask her outright?' she suggested.

'I could, but she's likely to stick to her original story, that he's done some work for her friend.'

'Ask Dad?'

Jack gave a harsh laugh. 'He's not going to admit to anything, is he?'

'This could all be totally innocent, Jack. Dad *will* have met a lot of people through his work,' conceded Natalie, ever the peacemaker.

'So why act so guiltily then?' he retorted. Then he added, 'And it's not like he hasn't got form, is it?'

'No,' she agreed dully. 'But I like to think that's all in the past.'

'*I'd* like to think it's all in the past,' answered Jack.

'Well.' Natalie sighed now. 'Time will tell. If there is something, it'll rear its head. It's bound to.'

All the way home Jack kept going over and over what he and Natalie had discussed. Before returning the phone to his parents' house, he parked up in a nearby sideroad and pulled it out of his jacket pocket. He knew the passcode to open it, his dad's date of birth, and was instantly in. Jack immediately clicked on 'contacts' and scoured down the list for Tara's name. Nothing. Then he went to 'messages' and quickly scanned what was there. Again, nothing of any consequence. Jack went to 'calls' but didn't see anything suspicious there either. Then, as an afterthought, he searched the missed calls and inhaled sharply. There it was, Tara's number.

Chapter 20

'There'll be over a hundred people coming!' gasped Emma. She was counting up the invites sent out, knowing only a few were unable to make the launch party and had given their apologies. Felix gave a lazy smile.

'Don't worry, it'll be fine,' he assured her. 'At least there's plenty of room.'

'Hmm, that's true,' she replied, looking around the spacious hall with its high cherry-yellow ceiling and marbled floor. A door with an art deco sunburst mantel led from it to the drawing room, which also held plenty of space. Emma could picture the scene now; glamorous people of the show rubbing shoulders with family and friends; a jazz band playing, cocktails flowing and then… the moment of anticipation, when the big screen Felix had hired was lit up with the opening credits of *Lady Scarlett Investigates*. A gush of excitement flooded Emma, not only because of the first ever episode's viewing, but also because of the theme tune she had sung the lyrics to.

Emma still had to pinch herself when thinking about it. For years she had sung in a band which her friends had formed. Together they had earned a good reputation locally and were often busy, usually in the summer months gigging in pubs, outside venues or festivals. Felix had suggested Emma sing the *Lady Scarlett Investigates* theme song at a meeting with the music director, who had wanted jaunty lyrics to accompany the upbeat tune. Emma had been a real hit in the studios and had proved more than capable. Now, here she was, after years of wanting to make it in the music world, her voice was about to sing to the nation. Or, as Felix kept pointing out, the world, if the copyrights to the show were sold worldwide. It was a happy yet daunting prospect, and Emma couldn't help but feel gratitude to Felix for creating the opportunity.

He in return was just plain relieved his girlfriend was content to stay with him, helping to look after this huge house he'd bought, rather than go off touring with her band.

Felix had fallen in love instantly with both the art deco house and Emma, who had passed his PA's interview with flying colours. She had applied for the housekeeping position, curiosity getting the better of her. Not only had Emma always admired the big house on the peninsula in Samphire Bay, but she'd been equally intrigued (as all had in Samphire Bay) as to who had bought the place. On being offered the position, Felix had introduced himself – much to her shock and amazement.

Fortunately, Emma's level-headed and grounded disposition had meant a good working relationship had easily developed, which soon merged into a personal one. It hadn't taken long for all to see the attraction between the two. Polly Andrews, the actress playing Lady Scarlett, had particularly teased the two of them, with her knowing looks and cheeky remarks. She had labelled Emma 'the real lady of the house' on one occasion, making Emma blush furiously.

Now though, after the first series had been filmed, Felix and Emma's relationship was public knowledge. The cast and film crew all knew and liked Emma, having known her from the start. It had been Emma who had looked after them from day one, serving their refreshments and guiding them around the house. Nobody knew every nook and cranny like she did. But most of all, Emma was popular for her down-to-earth manner and easy way about her. There were no airs or graces, just a natural charm, which was precisely why Felix fell for her in the first place, along with her beautiful warm amber eyes and flowing chestnut curls. And, in turn, Emma had been smitten with her tall, dark, handsome boss, with his olive complexion and friendly approach. Felix had never treated her as staff, but almost as a member of family, especially as his French mother, Madeleine, had taken a shine to her.

'You have chosen well, *mon chéri*,' she'd commented. Felix knew damn well it wasn't just the house she'd been referring to. For all the couple's pretence of a purely professional relationship, it had been blatantly clear to all those around them that it *so* wasn't. The magnetism between them was palpable.

Nobody had been more pleased to learn that Felix and Emma were officially a couple than Madeleine. And nobody more devastated than Felix's supermodel ex-girlfriend, Anika Genness, who was thankfully now behind bars. Anika had taken stalking to new limits, until finally attempting to physically harm Emma. It had been a traumatic time for them to say the least, which was why Felix had been determined to throw the mother of all launch parties. It was the first drama he had directed and they deserved to celebrate in style, after all they'd been through.

He looked at Emma, her eyes darting around the hall, assessing what needed doing. In many ways she was still the housekeeper, point blankly refusing to hire anyone else in her place. And why should she? Emma knew this house like the back of her hand and was happy to remain in charge of it. He grinned to himself, knowing she'd have everything under control.

'I'm thinking...' she said with narrowed eyes.

'Yes?'

'Of drinks and canapes on the lawn to start with, then all being seated here, in the hall, with the big screen over there.' She pointed to the sweeping staircase.

'Good idea,' he agreed. 'The acoustics will be fantastic in here.'

'Absolutely,' gushed Emma, knowing how well the grand piano sounded reverberating around the marbled hall, which then reminded her. 'We'll have to move the piano, make maximum room.'

'No problem. We'll transfer it to the library. Nobody will be going in there.'

Emma nodded in reply.

'Although, I was hoping you might play it at some point?' Felix suggested with a raised eyebrow.

'No,' she replied firmly. 'You'll all hear my voice singing the theme tune, that's enough.'

He came and wrapped his arms around her and placed his lips over hers.

'Never enough,' he whispered in her ear, making her giggle in delight.

'Which room shall I put Dad and Bunty in?' Emma, ever practical, had moved back onto the arrangements, totally ruining the moment for Felix.

'What?'

'Dad and Bunty, they'll be stopping over, so they can both relax and have a drink. We discussed this, remember?' She searched his face with those stunning amber eyes.

'Did we?' He scratched his head, not recalling this conversation at all. He remembered her saying his mother would be in the Rose Room…

'*Yes,*' insisted Emma.

'Oh, well, whichever room you think best,' he said, wondering how his mum and Emma's dad would get along. Probably fine, he thought, although they did both speak their minds. Even so, they were bound to meet at some point, better sooner than later, he concluded.

'It'll be fine, you know.' It was Emma's turn to reassure him now. He frowned slightly. 'Having our parents here, it'll be fun.'

He gave a slight snigger. 'I hope so.'

''Course it will!' she cheered. 'Your mum's great company and my dad's—'

'Overprotective?' butted in Felix with a smirk.

'Just being a dad, that's all. Bunty will keep him in check,' she smiled. True, her dad was protective of her, but he'd been a single parent since she was thirteen, so it was probably inevitable. 'He still likes you.' She nudged him playfully.

'Good to know,' he said with a wink. 'Because I'm not going anywhere.' He wrapped her in his arms tightly once more.

Chapter 21

Jasmine stood in the nursery glancing around its cream walls dotted with bright, colourful pictures. Then her eyes cast over the two matching cots, stood side by side next to the window. She took a deep breath and gently rubbed her now very swollen belly.

'Not long to go,' she whispered to the two babes inside her.

Jasmine had been told by the midwife that it was expected for twins to arrive much earlier than a single baby. With that in mind, both she and Robin were relieved that they'd finished the nursery in good time. She was finding it rather tiring and difficult to get about now, so much so, Robin was concerned. He was especially uneasy about the up-and-coming launch party they'd been invited to. He entered the nursery with a pained expression.

'Do you think it's wise to go?' he asked, holding the invitation in his hand.

'Oh, Robin, don't fuss. I'll be perfectly fine,' she replied, half expecting this.

'Are you sure?' Robin's face etched with anxiety. 'It *is* on the peninsula. What if—?'

'Honestly, I'll be fine,' interrupted Jasmine a touch impatiently, then immediately felt guilty for being so sharp with him. She was tired and irritable. Being so big and uncomfortable didn't allow much sleep. 'Sorry.' She went to give him a hug – well, as best as she could being the size she was. 'I don't mean to sound so snappy,' she consoled.

'I know.' He rubbed her back in an attempt to comfort her.

'I just want them born safely… and soon,' Jasmine whimpered, on the verge of tears, which wasn't helping Robin's stress levels.

'Oh, Jas…' He too was filled with emotion.

Then they were distracted by a voice calling from the garden below. They both looked out of the window to see Bunty waving up at them. For the first time ever, Jasmine resented her neighbour's interruption. She just wanted peace and quiet at the moment and sensed Robin felt the same, judging by his impatient sigh.

'I don't want company right now,' she said tearfully, not at all like her usual self. Robin understood. It was part and parcel of the pregnancy and he totally respected the hormones that must be rife, circulating round her system.

'I'll deal with it,' he replied gently, then made his way downstairs. After opening the back door, he told Bunty – as diplomatically as possible – now wasn't a good time.

'I see.' She nodded sagely, not in the least offended, then bid him goodbye. Robin was relieved by Bunty's reaction, not wanting to upset their dear elderly neighbour. But it did also give him food for thought. Was it going to work out having such a close friend living right next door? In many ways they considered themselves very fortunate to have Bunty as their neighbour, but now he was beginning to realise it may also prove a tad intrusive. Bunty was renowned for her forthright opinions and meddlesome ways. In fact, it had been Bunty's 'meddling' that had brought him and Jasmine together. Deciding they would make a perfect couple, Bunty had instigated circumstances leading them to meet. For that alone, he'd be eternally grateful, but now he had a pregnant girlfriend to think of and didn't want her at the neighbour's beck and call. Jasmine needed rest. And rest was what she was going to get.

He went back upstairs to the nursery to join her, but she wasn't there. Instead he found Jasmine lying on their bed, fast asleep. He smiled to himself and softly sat next to her on the edge. He watched in wonder as her bump slowly rose and fell. It seemed incredible to think it held his two children and tried to picture what they'd look like. Dark-haired like him, or blonde like their mother? It could even be one of each, he thought with a chuckle.

Robin was glad they didn't know the sex of their babies. He'd understood why Jasmine had thought it far more practical to know and prepare for them, but he wanted the surprise. It also meant they'd had to choose both male and female names. They still hadn't narrowed them down yet, finding it difficult to agree on one name, let alone two. So far they'd ruled out any of their family names, wanting to go for something a little more unusual, rather than traditional names.

'I fancy something a bit different, not run of the mill,' remarked Jasmine. Robin had raised an eyebrow. He'd been more concerned about their children's surname more than anything. When he'd said as much, Jasmine had frowned.

'Spencer, of course,' she'd said, matter of fact. They were planning on getting married after all, so why not? Robin was glad. It had crossed his mind she may have wanted a double-barrelled surname which included her own. But yes, he agreed it made sense just to use his name, as Jasmine would indeed become a Spencer too. This then led to the next thing on Robin's mind – marriage. *When* exactly would they be tying the knot? He didn't want the issue of marriage getting lost in the midst of caring for two young newborns. Left to him, he'd have done it months ago, but it had been Jasmine who had insisted on not rushing. He could see it from her point of view, but a part of him wished they'd just done it. Basically, Robin merely wanted his little family wrapped tightly all together, safe and sound. And who could blame him?

–

Bunty returned home, hoping Jasmine was OK. It wasn't like her friend not to want visitors, but then she must be tired, she acknowledged. As Jasmine and Robin's next-door neighbour, Bunty was used to calling unannounced whenever the mood took her. Now it looked as though that was about to change. Of course things were going to be different, thought Bunty. Whereas Jasmine had been a young, free woman, ready to share chit-chat and gossip over a coffee, now she was about to become a mother to two tiny babies. In short, her friend's priorities were about to change – big time. Instead of feeling any form of sadness, Bunty envisaged a happy future, seeing the babies growing up next door to her. She imagined twin prams on the lawn, toddlers playing in the sand, children splashing in the sea, cries of 'Auntie Bunty!' to come and join them… She couldn't wait. Then her thoughts turned to Perry. Would Emma have babies soon too, making him a granddad? The anticipation filled her with joy and excitement. They may be in the autumn of their life, but the future looked bright. Bright indeed.

'OK, love? Was Jasmine not in?' asked Perry as Bunty entered the kitchen.

'Yes, but she's tired and a little fragile at the moment,' she replied.

'Oh, I see,' he said. Then added, 'Nothing's wrong though, is there?'

'No, no.' Bunty shook her head.

'Well, she's not long to go now, has she?' asked Perry.

'Definitely not. In fact, I think it's imminent,' said Bunty warily, hoping and praying her friend was going to be all right.

'So, soon we'll have two new neighbours then?' Perry laughed.

She faced him with a smile. How much her life had changed. Over a year ago, she'd been living alone, almost as a recluse, in a huge house that was cut off by the tide twice daily. Absolute seclusion. It beggared belief to think she now had a husband, a stepdaughter, two lovely neighbours and was about to have two babies enter her life. A warm surge of happiness swept through her. Yes, the future looked rosy indeed.

Chapter 22

Emma was at fever pitch. She was overseeing the catering staff in the kitchen, making sure all the canapes were prepared and the bubbly perfectly chilled. Thankfully, everything was in order. The clock chiming told her the launch party would be starting in approximately half an hour.

'If you could start to bring the glasses and champagne onto the lawn, that would be great,' she instructed the staff, wanting their guests to be greeted in style.

Felix, meanwhile, was in the hall, testing out the large screen that had been installed. Situated centrally by the entrance to the staircase, it meant that everybody would have a good view. They'd had to hire chairs to seat all attending. Sound reverberated from the speakers he'd set around the marbled hall, bringing the place to life. Excellent, thought Felix, this was exactly what he'd been at pains to create. He so wanted the first episode of his first-ever drama to sound pitch perfect. He also wanted Emma's voice to shine too, knowing what a huge deal it was to her – and him.

'Everything on track?' he asked as Emma came up the kitchen stairs to join him.

'Yep, all good. What about here? Is it working all right?' She nodded towards the screen.

'Certainly is,' he replied, then checked his watch. 'Come on, they'll be arriving soon.' He took her hand and together they made their way to the grounds outside to meet their guests.

As predicted, the coaches carrying the film cast, crew and production team arrived first. It pleased Felix that they were the earliest. It was, after all, a party to celebrate their hard work. Out they poured, full of spirit and cheer, excited to see the start of *Lady Scarlett Investigates*. As director, Felix had naturally seen the complete series, but the actors and crew hadn't seen a full episode yet, only dailies from scenes made on the day. Felix knew they wouldn't be disappointed. It was a fine production and one they should all be very proud of.

'Hello and welcome!' gushed Emma, running to meet them. The catering staff were well trained and made sure everyone had drinks.

Polly Andrews wove through the crowd to seek out Emma. Felix had brought Polly from London to Samphire Bay to stay a few days in his home before filming, to introduce Polly to her surroundings and give her a sense of familiarity. Being a similar age to Emma, and also sharing the same mischievous sense of humour, the two had much in common. Many a time they'd be seen huddled together, whispering, gossiping and chuckling.

'Emma!' Polly cried, arms outstretched.

'Polly!' Emma hugged her friend in glee.

'I can't wait to see it,' trilled Polly, then hastily added, 'and hear your voice.'

'I know! It all feels a little surreal, doesn't it?' Emma instantly cringed. Of course it wouldn't feel surreal to Polly, she was a well-known actress.

Polly grinned and hooked arms with her. 'You're going to wow them all,' she said with a wink.

Next to arrive was Jennifer, Felix's PA, along with her husband. Felix was glad she hadn't made the trip from London alone, knowing how she had resented having to travel to Samphire Bay initially.

'Jennifer, good to see you, and you too, Alan,' he said, kissing her cheek and shaking hands with her husband.

'Fantastic place you've got here, Felix,' remarked Alan, gazing out at the bay.

'It is. We're very lucky,' he replied.

Jennifer's mouth twitched at the reference to *we're* lucky, not *I'm* lucky. So, he and Emma were obviously going strong then.

Felix scanned the crowd. He knew his mother's flight was on time and he'd sent a taxi to meet her at the airport. He noticed Perry and Bunty arrive and went to greet them.

'Hi, Perry, Bunty.'

Perry nodded in acknowledgment, while Bunty's eyes darted around the lawn, which was buzzing with activity.

'My, my, I've never seen such a star-studded crowd. Is that Brian Chapman?' she gasped, recognising the famous actor.

'Yes. I'll introduce you, if you want?' laughed Felix, earning a sly grin from Perry.

'Oh, would you?' gushed Bunty.

'Felix, *mon chéri*!' called a lovingly familiar voice. He whipped around to face his mother.

'Oh, Mum.' He hugged her hard. 'Meet Emma's dad, Perry, and his wife, Bunty.'

'*Enchanté*,' said Madeleine with a charming smile.

'Pleased to meet you,' they both replied in unison. They were soon joined by Emma.

'Come through,' she said. 'I'll show you to your rooms.'

It still felt odd to Bunty to be 'shown' into the house, like she didn't know every nook and cranny of her childhood home. Felix took his mother's suitcase and walked behind them. A touch of foreboding prickled him, hoping his mum, Perry and Bunty were all going to get along.

The last of the guests included Jasmine and Robin. Robin still had grave reservations about Jasmine being out at all, let alone at a busy party. But, as usual, Jasmine had insisted she was fine and wouldn't be put off. Reluctantly, Robin had driven them slowly down the tidal road and helped an ever-expanding, panting Jasmine up the steps to the house.

As for Jack and Tara, well, that had been quite another ordeal. As expected, and on form, Richard had tried his best to ruin things. Tara anticipated some kind of disruption, especially as he'd seen the party invite. On cue, just as she was about to drop Calum off as arranged, Richard had rung to say he couldn't have him. Something 'urgent' had cropped up and it just wasn't convenient for Calum to stay that weekend. Tara didn't even bother to ask what the so-called catastrophe was, knowing the answer would all be lies. Instead, she rolled her eyes and made a curt response, followed by a slam of the phone. Dully accepting she wouldn't be able to make the party, she rang Jack to explain. However, Jack was having none of it.

'Bring Calum then. I'm sure it'll be fine,' he'd replied, whilst trying to contain his anger. What an absolute prick this Richard sounded like.

'You sure?' asked Tara, secretly delighted at Jack's suggestion.

'Of course,' he assured, not really caring if it was or not. Frankly, he couldn't give a damn. There was no way Tara was missing out on this party. And no way was he showing up on his own either.

Calum had whooped with joy when Tara had told him to get his glad rags on.

So, here they were, all three of them, a tad late, but eager to join the party. Emma had made them welcome and dutifully made a fuss of Calum.

'Come and meet Felix,' she said with a grin, making Calum's eyes widen in awe.

'Really?' he asked. Tara and Jack exchanged a knowing smile.

'And Tara too, she's a huge fan,' teased Jack, making Tara blush.

'Shush, Jack.' She elbowed him, then quickly intervened as Calum picked up a glass of champagne from a passing tray. 'No, Calum.' She took the glass firmly from him with a shake of her head.

'Come on, Calum, let's find you something to drink,' said Emma and led him away.

Tara sighed happily and took in her surroundings.

'I can't believe I'm here,' she whispered, taking a sip of champagne.

Jack smiled fondly, loving her reaction. He was glad they'd brought Calum along to the party, it had proved to be a good icebreaker when being introduced to him. As first impressions go, Jack had surpassed himself. Calum had regarded him as 'cool', much to his satisfaction. It had also opened his eyes though, as to what he was going to have to deal with. A spiteful ex-husband. Clearly Richard played dirty and put his own selfish jealousy before any chance of Tara's happiness. Hadn't she been through enough?

Determined not to let Tara's ex ruin their afternoon, Jack made sure her glass was always full and introduced her to Jasmine.

'So pleased to meet you,' she smiled and shook Tara's hand.

'All settled in then?' asked Robin with a grin.

'Yes, thanks. Calum loves the apartment,' replied Tara, all the while clocking how tired his girlfriend looked. Should she really be here on her feet? They were interrupted by Felix's voice.

'If you'd like to make your way into the hall, *Lady Scarlett Investigates* is about to start!' he announced, causing a flurry of activity.

Everyone scuttled inside in search of a good seat. Emma had wisely reserved the first two rows for family and friends.

'I'll sit at the end of the row,' said Jasmine.

'Good idea, there'll be more room,' answered Robin.

Tara overheard and thought it sensible, suspecting Jasmine may need a hasty exit. Once all settled, a silent anticipation fell amongst the audience. Then the big screen lit up into life and the title '*Lady Scarlett Investigates*' blazed across it, accompanied by the catchy, upbeat theme tune.

Emma closed her eyes and held her breath – there it was, her voice!

'Lady Scarlett, super sleuth,
With her emerald eyes and raven hair,
She'll figure it out,
Without a doubt,

Such a quick mind and elegant flair!

Lady Scarlett is on the trail,
Hunting for clues and fingerprints,
She's on the case,
Looking for a trace,
The culprit will get caught in a jinks!'

Perry was filled with emotion at hearing his daughter's voice and gulped back the lump in his throat. Jasmine was also gulping, but not with emotion.

'Robin,' she hissed in his ear, 'my waters have broken.'

Before Robin could respond, Tara, who had been keeping one eye on the screen and one on Jasmine, had witnessed the whole thing, and, being a doctor, began to take control.

'This way,' she quietly urged.

Together with Robin, they carefully led Jasmine to the drawing room.

'I need to get to the hospital,' she yelped breathlessly.

Robin stared out of the window in panic.

'The tide's in!' he croaked with alarm.

Chapter 23

'I'm ringing the air ambulance,' stated Tara calmly, reaching for her phone. Jack had followed them into the drawing room and was looking as terrified as Robin.

'How long will it take to come?' he asked under his breath.

'They'll be here soon,' replied Tara firmly. Within seconds she was giving concise details of the situation and their whereabouts.

Jasmine sat panting rapidly on the sofa with Robin crouched in front of her, clasping her hand.

'It's going to be OK, Jas,' he valiantly attempted to soothe, when inside he was crashing. He cursed himself for driving them here. They should never have come in the first place.

Perspiration poured from Jasmine's face as she continued to take great gulps of air. Tara went to sit next to her and put a hand on her forehead. She was burning up and badly needed assistance.

'The ambulance is on its way,' she assured her. 'We'll soon have you safe and sound.'

She quickly pulled up a footstool and gently helped Jasmine put her legs up. Then she checked her pulse, which was racing. Her eyes scanned the room frantically. If needs be, the ambulance crew may have to deliver the babies on site, depending on how advanced Jasmine's labour was. At least she'd be on hand to help.

After what seemed an agonising wait, help was soon on its way. To their utter relief, they heard it, the helicopter blades whooshing in the distance.

'It's here!' yelled Jack, running to the bow window.

'Thank God!' cried Robin, on the verge of tears.

Outside in the hall, the volume was so loud on the big screen, and the audience so gripped with the drama, that only when the helicopter landed on the lawn did they notice it, causing a commotion.

Emma and Felix dashed to the drawing room to see the patio doors flung open and the air ambulance crew carrying Jasmine out to the helicopter on a stretcher, with a now frantic Robin scurrying behind. Tara appeared totally in control, giving the paramedics information, marching alongside them. She got into the helicopter too while Jack nodded and gave the thumbs-up to her. And then they were gone, whisked away to the hospital.

Emma and Felix stared in shock, dumbfounded. Jack walked back through the patio doors into the drawing room, white as snow.

'Jack, what happened?' gasped Emma, eyes wide.

'Jasmine's waters broke. She's gone into labour,' replied Jack, then puffed his cheeks out.

'Oh, my God, is she OK?' she asked urgently.

'Hopefully. She's in safe hands,' said Jack, all the time admiring Tara's composed direction of the situation. What a woman. They were then interrupted by a puzzled-looking Calum.

'Where's Mum?' He frowned.

'It's all right, mate,' answered Jack and told him what had happened and where Tara was. Calum, like the others, had been so engrossed with the big screen that he'd missed seeing his mum disappear with Jasmine and Robin. Felix looked from Jack to Emma, not really knowing what to say. There was a moment's hiatus.

'Your mum will ring me as soon as there's news,' stated Jack.

'OK.' Calum nodded. Then asked, 'Can I watch the rest of the programme?'

Jack smirked at this coolness. Clearly Calum took after his mum.

'I don't see why not.' He shrugged. 'We can't do anything else, can we?'

—

Jasmine was wheeled swiftly and smoothly into the maternity ward, where a consultant and two nurses stood waiting for her. Tara was on hand again, giving details that Robin frustratingly couldn't understand. He was struggling to take everything in. Talk of blood pressure, heartbeats, IV fluids, gas, air and incubators were banded about. 'It's my fault,' he kept telling himself. He should have insisted they stayed at home, not having his girlfriend on her feet. His thoughts flashed back to helping Jasmine up the steps to Felix's house. What fools they'd been! He should have insisted, put his foot down, been *adamant* that she stayed at home and rested.

Looking at her now though, she did seem calmer, breathing deeply, steadily, instead of feverishly panting. She was being given calm instructions, and as the remarkable, pragmatic, *wonderful* woman she was, Jasmine took everything in her stride. His heart burst with pride. 'Pull yourself together, Spencer,' he now told himself. He had to be strong to support her. She was the one going through it all, led on a bed, being examined, assessed and God knows what else. Robin closed his eyes. Get a grip, man, his inner voice ordered. And he did. He held his amazing woman's hand throughout the short but intense labour.

As the babies were premature, as expected, they were tiny and delivered with ease. The complicated part was the care they'd need after birth. The two small incubators at the foot of the bed lay waiting to whiz the newborns to the neonatal unit. A boy came first, fists clenched, feet kicking and wailing like a banshee, followed by his sister, whose cries were a touch more subdued. Tears poured down Robin's face as he watched them being carefully transported and nestled safely into incubators. Then his eyes swept to Jasmine, looking exhausted but happy. She too was crying.

'Let me see them,' she softly called.

'Of course,' said the consultant with a smile.

Jasmine slightly raised herself as her tiny twins were wheeled closer. Still holding Robin's hand, they exchanged a look of pure love.

'We'll get them into neonatal. You'll be able to join them shortly,' comforted one of the nurses.

'Thank you so much,' croaked Robin.

Tara was sat outside anxiously waiting. As the babies passed her, she quickly got up and rushed to speak to the nurses. Recognising Dr O'Hara, they quickly filled her in whilst rushing to neonatal. Tara took a deep breath and made her way back to the labour ward. After half an hour, when Jasmine had been looked over, she tapped on the door and poked her head round. She saw Jasmine and Robin still clutching hands, looking both tired and jubilant.

'Congratulations,' she said, smiling warmly.

'Tara, I can't thank you enough,' sobbed Jasmine.

'Don't mention it. That's my job!'

'We've a boy and a girl,' she gushed with glee.

'I know. I've just seen them,' replied Tara, suddenly feeling emotional too. Then she took in Robin, still pale and dazed. 'You OK, Robin?'

He looked up, eyes still watery. 'I'm the proudest man alive,' he answered gruffly.

—

Jack had taken Calum back to Tara's home and was waiting on tenterhooks for her call.

'I'm hungry,' complained Calum.

'Pizza?' suggested Jack. He too was feeling peckish, having only had a few canapes all day.

'Yeah!' cheered Calum.

'OK, I'll order. What do you fancy?'

'Hot spicy beef,' answered Calum instantly. This new fella of Mum's was really beginning to grow on him.

'Coming up,' said Jack, scrolling through his contacts for the local pizza delivery. After ordering, the landline phone rang. Calum answered it.

'Hi, Mum.' Jack's head darted towards him. 'Yeah, I'll put him on.' Then Calum passed the phone.

'Hi.'

'Hi, Jack, I just tried your mobile, but it was engaged.'

'I've just been ordering pizzas. Everything OK?' he asked anxiously.

'Yes. A boy and a girl, safely delivered, and two very happy parents,' replied Tara.

'Oh, thank God.'

'I'm on my way home now. Thanks for taking care of Calum.'

'No worries,' said Jack.

'Bye, won't be long.'

'OK, see ya.'

Jack smiled as he put the phone down, pleased to be of help. Then it rang again. He grinned, figuring it was probably Tara wanting pizza too. He should have thought to ask her. He picked up the receiver, expecting to hear her voice. Instead he got an irate male one.

'Where the hell have you been?' thundered the voice. Jack blinked. 'Try answering your phone!'

Jack paused before answering. 'I take it you want to speak to Tara.' He spoke in a cold, rigid tone. There was a deathly silence.

'Who is this?' hissed the voice.

'None of your goddamn business,' replied Jack, then put the phone down. So, that was Richard. What a dickhead.

Chapter 24

Jack had rung Bunty to tell her the good news.

'A boy and a girl!' she'd exclaimed, absolutely delighted.

Although Jack was thrilled about his friend's babies, his mood was tainted a little by Tara's ex-husband's behaviour. It had left him feeling a mixture of things. Anger certainly, but most of all concern. The alpha male in him wanted to protect Tara. Richard clearly had a temper, and this worried Jack.

When he'd relayed the conversation back to Tara, she'd merely rolled her eyes.

'Yeah, that sounds about right,' she'd said witheringly.

This disturbed Jack further. Obviously she was used to being treated and spoken to so badly. Not wanting to make too much of an issue, he refrained from discussing it further. He remembered her reluctance to talk about her marriage in The Smugglers, so didn't press it. But the questions he badly wanted to ask Tara were mounting up, and not just concerning her ex-husband. Why did you ring my dad? topped the list. But for now he'd bide his time. He was a patient man and would strike when the timing was right.

Bunty announced the birth of Jasmine and Robin's twins to all that evening, after Jack had rung her. Once the launch party ended and everyone had left, Emma cooked supper for her guests and they raised a glass to toast the babies' safe arrival.

'Bless them,' said Bunty with a tear in her eye.

'What a dramatic start,' replied Emma, so relieved to hear that the newborns and Jasmine were all doing fine.

'All is well that ends well. Isn't that what you English say?' asked Madeleine with an arched eyebrow.

'Thanks to Tara,' replied Felix gravely.

'Yes, thank God a doctor was in the house.' Bunty gulped, not bearing to think of what might have happened.

'Well, one was and she handled the situation marvellously,' comforted Perry, patting her shoulder, 'and we'll be meeting our new little neighbours soon, I'm sure.'

This caused Madeleine to frown, confused by Perry's words.

'Bunty and Perry live next door to Jasmine and Robin,' explained Felix to his mother.

'Ah! *Je vois*. It will be lovely having babies about, *non*?' cheered Madeleine, then cheekily winked at Emma.

Emma blinked. What was that supposed to mean? Was Felix's mum inferring something? She looked towards her dad who grinned knowingly. It hadn't been lost on him either. Felix clocked the interaction and quickly changed the subject.

'So, what did we think of *Lady Scarlett Investigates* then?' he asked.

'Brilliant!' gushed Emma. 'I knew it would be.' She beamed at him.

'*Excellente*. You did a good job there, *mon chéri*,' said Madeleine, raising her glass to him.

'Absolutely,' agreed Perry, who hadn't actually expected to enjoy it so much. Then he quickly added,

'And Emma, you sang the theme tune beautifully.' He faced his daughter with a warm smile.

'She has the voice of an angel,' stated Felix, not for the first time.

'Oh, stop,' replied Emma laughing happily. Secretly she was praying that the drama would sell worldwide. Hopefully, this could open all kinds of doors for her in the music world. Never had she dared to dream of such things.

Robin was thinking something similar as he gazed into the two incubators. His heart burst with love as he watched his son and daughter sleeping peacefully, despite the many tubes coming from their tiny bodies. They'd had quite a day. Their dramatic arrival had raised everybody's heart rate, including their own. Robin had heard the consultant's concern after he'd monitored Jasmine when they first arrived at the hospital. It was a blessing they'd been born so shortly afterwards. Robin was only just coming to terms with what could so easily have gone catastrophically wrong. It made him sick to his stomach contemplating it. But, he reminded himself, it hadn't. Thanks to Tara's efficiency and Jasmine's steadiness, plus the amazing hospital staff, they'd got through it. He shuddered and closed his eyes. *Never* would he allow Jasmine or his children to come under such threat again. He glanced over the incubators once more before leaving to join Jasmine in the ward. She was just stirring from a doze and smiled drowsily at seeing him sit by her bedside.

'They're sleeping peacefully,' Robin told her.

'Good.' She yawned and sat up.

'We'll have to decide on names,' said Robin.

'Well, I've been thinking...' replied Jasmine tentatively.

'Oh yeah?' He grinned, knowing where this was going. He knew Jasmine wanted unusual names, not 'run of the mill' as she'd put it. Personally, he'd be happy to call his daughter Tara, such was his appreciation towards her.

'Hmm, I thought Jemima for our daughter?' suggested Jasmine.

'Jemima?' replied Robin in surprise. This was one she hadn't mentioned before. But yes, he quite liked it. Jemima Spencer... Yes, it sounded good. 'That's nice.' He nodded in approval. 'What about our son's name?'

'I'd like to name him after the consultant,' said Jasmine firmly.

'Good idea,' agreed Robin before asking, 'what's his name?'

'Barnaby.'

Robin paused. Barnaby? He looked into Jasmine's searching eyes. Could he deny her anything?

'OK... Could we shorten it maybe?'

'To Barny?'

Now that's more like it, thought Robin.

'Hmm, Barny Spencer, I rather like that,' he said with a laugh. He imagined a mischievous little boy with an impish smile.

'It sounds... cute, doesn't it?' chuckled Jasmine.

'Cool,' corrected Robin. 'Barny and Jemima, cool dudes.' He winked.

'Cool dudes,' agreed Jasmine with utter joy.

After all the commotion of the day, it was hardly surprising that everyone slept well that night. As Emma and Felix wearily climbed the stairs, they were glad to be finally getting some rest. Their guests had retired hours ago, while they'd sat up with a night cap, reflecting on the day's events. Even though the launch party had been somewhat interrupted, it hadn't detracted from the reception Felix's drama had received. The first episode of *Lady Scarlett Investigates* had gone down a treat. He only hoped that the infamous critics would react the same way. As this was his first stab at directing, it was important to him that his work was well recognised, especially as he wanted to continue with directing, rather than acting again.

Emma was shattered. Playing hostess, as the lady of the house, was tiring work. But then, as the former house-keeper, she was used to it. She was just glad to be heading to Felix's bedroom, instead of her old one. Ironically, that's where her dad and Bunty were sleeping tonight.

It had felt strange to Bunty being directed to that bedroom, instead of turning left on the landing where her bedroom since childhood had been. To Perry, it felt bizarre to be staying in the big white house at all. After being banned from the place a lifetime ago, it seemed surreal to be climbing up the sweeping staircase, where Bunty's father had once callously dismissed him.

Madeleine always slept like a log, tonight even more so. Her son had chosen well. Emma was the perfect match for him. Gone were the days when she worried about his previous toxic relationship. Ditching that obsessive mad woman had been the best thing Felix had ever done. Now she could look forward to grandchildren…

Not wanting to drive home and leave Jasmine and the twins that night, Robin had been offered a family room to sleep in at the hospital. Like Jasmine, he was soon out like a light. Meanwhile, Barny and Jemima quietly kept each other company, snuggled contently side by side.

Chapter 25

Tara opened the envelope, inwardly preparing herself. She'd been expecting to hear from the court with a hearing date. Claire had warned her it was imminent. Even while knowing what lay ahead, Tara still stared at the letter a little daunted. It was all there, in black and white, the procedure she herself had instigated. Her and Richard's finances were about to be assessed by a District Judge, who would decide on the full and final settlement of the divorce. Long overdue in Tara's eyes – and Claire's.

'Honestly, I don't know what took you so long,' Claire said when she'd rung to tell her the letter had arrived.

'I know,' sighed Tara, 'but he'd worn me down so much, I just didn't have the energy to fight him.'

'Or the confidence. Never forget how he made you feel,' retorted Claire with bitterness in her voice. She had witnessed first-hand the decline and low self-esteem of her friend. It sickened her. It *enraged* her to think how Richard had slowly but surely sapped Tara of the spark and spirit she used to have. It was such a waste. Tara had been popular at university, sought after, until that manipulating ex-husband of hers had staked his claim.

Claire had always been suspicious of Richard. It amazed her how she seemed to be the only one who could see straight through him. While the rest of their housemates had revered the handsome, charming, soon-to-be dentist, Claire had immediately seen how he'd controlled Tara. The way he had 'helped' with her studies and cooked her meals just meant she never saw her friends. He managed to keep Tara to himself, instead of letting her live a normal, sociable student life. When Claire had learned of Tara's pregnancy, she hadn't been shocked. In fact, if anything, she'd seen it coming. Knowing that Richard had discouraged Tara from going on the pill, assuring her he'd 'take care of things', meant he'd had overall control of matters. Claire, rightly or wrongly, had suspected he'd been careless deliberately, in order to get Tara pregnant. He wanted Tara, and having his child meant he'd get her. And it had worked. Instead of her friend enjoying university years, she'd been pregnant, tired, stressed and most definitely Richard's.

'You'll be there, at court, won't you?' asked Tara.

'Of course. I'm representing you,' replied Claire. Then asked, 'Does Richard intend to get a solicitor?'

'I've no idea. I suspect he may want to represent himself. I think he still wants us to settle out of court, that he can win me round.'

Claire gave a harsh laugh. Those days were over. Then she paused, a slight dread seeped inside her.

'You won't let him persuade you into anything, will you?' she asked with trepidation.

'No, definitely not,' answered Tara firmly. She was doing this for Calum as much as herself. She was still smarting at how he was using their son as a pawn. Visions of an upset Calum sitting on his bedroom balcony flashed into her mind and her resolve strengthened. 'Absolutely no way.'

Claire nodded. 'Good.'

'So, will we meet before the hearing date?'

'No, I've got everything in order.' Too right. Claire had made it her personal mission to go through each document with a fine-tooth comb. She had studied every fact and figure meticulously. Doing so had only increased her hatred of Richard. The evidence before her had spelled out just how much he had got away with – up until now. Claire was about to uncover the injustices dealt to her friend. It was payback time. Richard was about to encounter her wrath. Claire was notorious for her thoroughness and persistence, as she liked to describe it. Her opponents in court had dubbed her 'The Rottweiler'.

'OK, thanks, Claire.'

'We'll just need to have a chat before the hearing starts, so get there an hour before,' she advised.

'Will do, and thanks again, Claire, for everything,' replied Tara with genuine gratitude.

'My pleasure,' replied Claire, totally meaning it.

Tara marked the calendar with the court date and made a mental note to check her hospital shifts. Not wanting Calum to know of the impending hearing, she simply drew a black star on the day. Then she wondered if Richard would tell him. How would he spin it? That Mum was dragging him to court in the hope of ripping him off? She wouldn't put it past him. But Calum was getting older and wiser. Tara doubted he'd swallow Richard's version of events now. Actions spoke louder than words, and Calum had seen Richard in action. He'd seen how his dad had left them, made his mum sell the family home, married the woman he'd had an affair with, and was about to start another family. They'd been cast aside.

Tara was also starting to doubt how happy Calum was staying at his dad's big new house, with his new young wife; his new, young, *pregnant* wife. Richard himself had told her Calum hadn't taken the pregnancy news well. How was he going to be when the baby was born? The more Tara considered it, the more convinced she was that Calum would gradually distance himself from Richard. Not that she particularly wanted it that way, but she could see the effect Richard's actions were having on their son.

On a brighter note, Tara was pleased that Calum's time with Jack had gone well. The two had gelled, much to her relief. Jack was the first man she'd introduced Calum to, and so had been slightly apprehensive. In a way, Richard had actually done them a favour. By refusing to have Calum, it meant that they had all gone to the launch party together, which had proved a natural, low-pressure way for the two to get to know each other. Calum had been totally awestruck with it all, especially meeting Felix Paschal. The fact Jack had connections to such celebrities had more than impressed him. Of course, all this would have been fed back to his dad. Now it was *his* turn to listen to how 'cool' mum's boyfriend was, instead of Tara having to stomach how wonderful Melissa was. Yes, the tables were well and truly turning.

Her thoughts were broken by a mobile call. It was Calum.

'Mum, can I stay at Ben's tonight?'

'Sure, if that's OK with Ben's mum?'

'Yeah, she's picking us up from school.'

'OK, what about tomorrow? Dad's supposed to be coming for you in the morning,' asked Tara, knowing it was Richard's weekend to have Calum. There was a pause.

'I don't want to go to Dad's. Can you pick me up from Ben's early evening tomorrow?'

Tara inwardly sighed. Her prediction was coming true.

'I will, but you need to contact Dad and let him know.' She certainly wasn't making the call.

'Yeah, I'll tell him,' he replied indifferently.

Well, why should he mind letting his dad down? thought Tara. It was only what Richard had done to him.

'OK love, see you tomorrow.'

'Bye, Mum!'

Chapter 26

Jack was thundering down the beach on his morning run. He was desperate to utilise all the pent-up energy building inside him. His head kept rewinding to that phone call off Tara's ex. He'd love to meet the man and give him a piece of his mind, but knew that would only cause more trouble for her. Instead, he'd decided to show support in any way he could. Also, what his sister had suggested a while ago had given him a lot to think about.

When Natalie had advised that he simply ask Tara if there was any connection to their dad, Jack had dismissed the idea. He'd said there'd be little point, as both had already brushed over the matter – somewhat lamely, in his opinion. But that was before he had seen Tara's missed call on his dad's mobile. That was cast iron proof that the two clearly *did* have some kind of association. Why lie? That was the question that really troubled Jack. Was there something ominous behind it all?

The more he mulled it over, the more puzzling it became. Yes, his dad did have a past, but he honestly seemed happy and content with his mum and had been for some time now. Ever since that horrendous period when his affair came to light, his parents had managed to patch up their marriage and stay strong together. And as for Tara, well, he really couldn't see her as 'the other woman'. It just didn't fit. Yet, ring him she did. *But why?*

was the burning question that Jack could not dismiss. He needed to address it. Come clean and tell Tara what he knew and ask her to explain. He had to. It was going to come between them if he didn't know, forever taunting him. In order for the relationship to progress, and he very much wanted it to, he had to get it out in the open.

Having made his decision, Jack slowed down and came to a halt. Leaning over and panting heavily, he waited for his heart rate and breathing to return to normal, then walked back up the beach to his house.

He felt better for having a plan and his mood lifted. His gaze spread over the turquoise bay, waves shimmering in the sunlight. He inhaled deeply, loving the moist, salty air. Looking to the sandy floor at the clumps of green samphire growing there, he bent down to pick some. Whilst deciding what to cook with it for dinner that night, an idea came to him. He'd invite Tara, and Calum too if he wasn't elsewhere.

Once home, he rang to see if she was free that evening.

'I am actually. Calum's at his friend's tonight,' she said, happy to accept his invitation.

'Good. Come about seven? Is that OK?'

'Great, thanks, see you then.'

So, maybe tonight would provide a good opportunity to confront her, thought Jack pensively.

—

Jack's jaw dropped when he opened the door to Tara a few hours later. Tara looked amazing. She wore an off-the-shoulder, green, silky top, with white, slim-line capri pants. The outfit complimented her svelte figure and emerald eyes.

'Hi.' She smiled, passing him a bottle of wine.

'Hi.' He gulped and stood aside to let her in.

All the time Tara was taking in his appearance and liked what she saw. Jack's wide shoulders and muscled biceps were evident in the black polo shirt he wore, as were his thick, strong thighs in the fitted black jeans.

'Something smells good,' she remarked, following him into the kitchen.

'Samphire and lemon salmon linguine,' said Jack, hovering over the oven. 'It should be ready in five minutes. Time for a drink first.' He took out a corkscrew from the kitchen drawer and proceeded to open the wine. After pouring it into two large glasses, he passed one to Tara. 'Cheers.' They clinked glasses.

'Cheers.' Tara took a large gulp. Hell, that hit the spot. 'So, how are the twins?' she asked with a smile.

'Oh, doing fine apparently. They're all Robin talks about these days,' he laughed.

Tara laughed too. 'Naturally.'

'I don't think it'll be too long before they can come home, according to him.'

'That's good news.'

'Yeah, it is, especially after their dramatic arrival.' He looked straight into those beautiful bright green eyes of hers. 'You do realise how tremendous you were that day, don't you?'

'Just doing my job,' she brushed away, a touch self-conscious.

'No, you saved the day, Tara,' he stated, still holding her gaze. Why couldn't she take praise? Had she been robbed of her self-worth? Once again his anger level started to simmer.

'How's the renovation coming along?' she asked, eager to change the subject.

'All good. It's gradually beginning to take shape. The first two apartments have all the internal walls in place,' replied Jack as he went back to the oven. 'It's ready. Let's eat.'

It didn't take them long to finish the meal. Both were hungry and relished it. Jack had surpassed himself.

Tara sat back with satisfaction. 'That was delicious,' she declared. It was a real treat to have a meal cooked for her. It had been some time since anyone had. Richard was a good cook too...

'OK?' asked Jack, seeing her face fall slightly.

Suddenly the stress of the forthcoming court proceedings crept up on her. Maybe because she'd had too much wine and allowed herself to relax for once, her inhibitions came tumbling down, and, to her horror, a tear escaped.

'Hey.' Jack rushed over and put his arm around her shoulders.

'S... sorry...' She quickly wiped away the tear.

'What is it, Tara?' he gently asked.

She met his gaze and shakily breathed in. 'I've... a court hearing.'

'Come on. Let's sit on the sofa.' Jack eased her up and led them to sit comfortably next to each other.

'This will explain things,' said Tara, grabbing the letter out of her bag. She'd kept it there, out of Calum's sight.

Jack read the letter with a grim expression. No wonder she was tense, with this hanging over her.

'Do you want me to come with you? As moral support?' he asked earnestly.

Why not? she thought. Why shouldn't she have Jack there to support her?

'Yes, I would,' she answered.

'Then I will.' He wrapped his arms tightly around her, all intentions of confronting her completely gone.

Chapter 27

Tara spent the next day glad to have had the apartment to herself. It was peaceful and gave her time and space to contemplate how kind Jack had been to her last night.

At eight o'clock in the evening, when it was time to pick Calum up from his friend's house, she tried his phone but there was no answer, so she grabbed her car keys and decided to just go there anyway.

However, on arriving, the door opened to a puzzled Ben.

'Hi, Ben, is Calum ready?' she asked.

'He left ages ago,' replied Ben.

'What? I was supposed to pick him up early evening,' said Tara with a frown. Then, seeing no response from him, she asked, 'When exactly did he leave?'

'About three hours ago,' came the reply.

Tara froze. *Three hours* ago. Where the hell was he?

'Did he say where he was going?' She forced herself to stay calm.

'No. Just thought he was going back home.'

'Can you think of anywhere he could be?' she asked in a choked voice.

'Err... Not really...'

They were interrupted by Ben's mum.

'Hi, Tara, come in.' She'd overheard the conversation. All three of them stood in the hallway. 'Listen, Ben, think carefully. Where would you guess Calum may have gone to?'

Ben shrugged his shoulders. 'I dunno. He never said he was going anywhere.'

Both women exchanged frantic looks.

'I'd better go home in case he's there.' Tara got in her car and drove at full pelt all the way back. The apartment was empty. Without hesitation, she rang Richard. To her annoyance, Melissa answered.

'Hello?' That sickly sweet voice irritated her further. Why was she answering Richard's mobile? Probably because it was her name flashing on his screen.

'I need to speak to Richard,' Tara said flatly.

'Oh, just a minute. I'll see if he's about...' He obviously was, as he came on immediately (and no doubt wasn't given chance to answer his own phone).

'Tara? What is it?'

'Calum's gone missing. I don't know where he is,' she stated.

There was a slight pause.

'Shit. Where was he?'

'At Ben's. I've just been there, and he said he left three hours ago,' she explained, her voice cracking with emotion.

'I'll have a drive around, see if I can see him. You stay home in case he returns.'

'Do you think I should ring the police?'

'Wait till I get there.'

'OK.' Down went the phone.

—

Jack too was reflecting on last night. Instead of feeling better about the situation with Tara, the evening had brought more complications than any form of clarification. Sighing, he decided to get a beer from the fridge. As he stood by the kitchen window tipping his bottle back, he caught sight of a flickering of light outside the window. Looking more closely, he saw a figure sat on a large rock by the side of the bay. They had just lit a cigarette. Who the hell was it? Jack didn't like the idea of some unknown hanging about near his house at this hour. He quickly made his way outside to face them.

The figure turned sharply at hearing him approach. Close up, Jack recognised him. It was Calum. Since when did *Calum* smoke?

'Calum, what are you doing here?' Jack asked quietly. Calum shrugged his shoulders and took a long drag of his cigarette. 'I take it your mum doesn't know where you are?' Calum shook his head and looked down. 'You better ring her. She'll be worried.' Still there was no reply. Jack went to sit on the rock next to him. 'What's the matter, Calum?' he gently asked feeling sorry for the lad.

'I'm sick of it all.'

'All what?'

'Them, Mum and Dad. I'm constantly stuck in the middle. Everything was fine until *she* came along.'

'She?'

'Melissa, dad's new wife. Dad's new *pregnant* wife.'

'Oh, I see.'

He stubbed his cigarette out with force. 'Dad's a dickhead.'

'Hmm,' Jack diplomatically offered, whilst secretly agreeing with him.

'Mel was all right at first. She couldn't do enough for me.' Then he gave a harsh laugh. 'But now I realise it was all an act, just to look good in front of Dad. As soon as her baby comes along, I'll be shoved out of the way.'

'I'm sure you won't, Calum.'

'I will. And do you know something else? Dad regrets the whole thing. It's obvious. It's written all over his face.' Another harsh laugh followed.

'We need to let your mum know where you are, mate.'

'Fine. You ring her then.'

Jack pulled out his mobile and made the call. Within a quarter of an hour, he was driving Calum safely home. Tara came rushing out down the corridor.

'Thanks so much, Jack,' she gushed while throwing her arms around her son.

'Just glad I saw him,' he replied, once more appreciating how much Tara had to contend with. Then his eyes moved to Richard, who was standing at Tara's door looking mutinous. He patted Calum on the back. 'See you around, buddy.'

'Thanks, Jack.' Calum gave him a half smile.

Jack leaned forward and whispered, 'Talk to your mum. And ditch the fags, mate, seriously.'

Tara overheard and gave him a questioning look. Jack winked reassuringly at her. 'I'll catch you tomorrow,' he mouthed. Tara nodded her head discreetly. He looked towards Richard again, who was staring stony-faced at him.

-

The next morning, Tara sat at the breakfast bar staring into space. She was on her second cup of coffee, waiting for Calum to put in an appearance. Already Richard had been hounding her with text messages, like she had all the answers.

> How is he? Keep me updated.

She was itching to speak to Jack, desperate to know the full details of exactly what had happened. It would be interesting to hear what he had to say, judging by his solemn expression, which was so unlike Jack. Plus, what he had whispered to Calum about talking to her? Surely Calum knew he could confide in his mum? Apparently not. Guilt started to edge its way in. *When* could her son sit down and talk to her? She was 'always at work' as he had recently commented. The coffee was starting to leave a bitter taste in her mouth. Her absence from the home was taking its toll. But what choice did she have? Someone had to keep the roof over their heads.

Her mind cast back to Richard and Melissa's new house with all the trimmings inside. Melissa didn't even work now. Once again, the injustice of it all stung hard. Again Tara reminisced the lifestyle they'd had as a family. Looking back, she now realised just how comfortable they had been; three holidays abroad a year, two in the summer and a winter break skiing; a beautiful, big Georgian home that she and Richard had enjoyed renovating together; an up-to-date wardrobe of clothes, not to mention the jewellery Richard often treated her to (that huge diamond engagement ring of Melissa's suddenly shot into focus). But what Tara missed most of all was the part-time working hours. She'd had the perfect work-life balance. It had given her the freedom to spend time at home with Calum, but also the interaction with colleagues and patients she craved.

Tara allowed herself to remember the good times as a family. There had been plenty, she reluctantly acknowledged. Saturday nights when the three of them shared a takeaway, chatting about the week they'd had, cheering Calum on from the sidelines while he played football, barbequing in the garden with neighbours, blasting out music and dancing into the early hours... The list was endless. And now look at them. They weren't a family any more. They were separated. Not talking. Richard was about to make a brand-new family.

She heard Calum slope into the kitchen and turned to face him.

'Coffee?' she asked with forced brightness.

'Thanks,' he mumbled and sat at the breakfast bar, knowing full well what was to come.

Tara placed his mug down in front of him. 'Calum, we need to talk, love.'

'Hmm,' came the reply.

'Why did you disappear like that? We were worried sick.'

'*We*? You might have been, but Dad couldn't care less.'

'You know that isn't true.'

'Do I?'

Tara opened her mouth to speak, then stopped, realising she didn't actually know what to say. After the thought pattern she'd just had, she could well see how Calum must feel. Hadn't she herself felt abandoned? They *had* been abandoned. Richard had chosen to leave them and start a new life with someone else. Why should she even start to defend him? A few moments passed in silence, as if each of them was absorbing the fact.

'Jack is all right, you know,' Calum eventually said somewhat matter of fact.

'Yes, he is,' she agreed.

There was another slight pause before Calum glanced sideways at her. 'You could do worse.'

'Sorry?' Tara asked in surprise.

'You and Jack.' He shrugged. 'Just saying.'

'Ah, I see,' she replied with an amused grin.

'Yeah, why not?'

Tara blinked. The sight of Jack's concerned face slid into her mind, as well as the compassion he'd previously shown her. There was clearly more to Jack than he initially let on.

'What are you thinking, Mum?' Calum eyed her pensively.

'Nothing!' she instantly answered, almost defensively.

'Honestly, if Dad can piss off with someone new then so should you.'

Tara resisted the urge to laugh. Then suddenly her face turned serious.

'Calum, I'd never leave, you know that?'

'I know. I just meant you deserve to be happy, Mum, that's all.'

Tara gulped. Now she was resisting the urge to cry. 'Knowing you're safe would make me happy, Calum.'

'Hmm.' He'd reverted back to monosyllabic replies.

'Which means no running off.'

Another grunt followed.

'And always talk to me. Tell me what's bothering you.'

Calum looked up. 'Dad being Dad bothers me. Why did he have to ruin everything?' Tara chewed her lip, again not knowing what to say. 'I thought he'd come back, you know.'

'Why?' She frowned.

'Because he looked miserable all of a sudden. I honestly thought he'd had enough of Mel. Then he announced he was going to be a dad again… and I realised she'd trapped him,' he choked, on the verge of tears.

'Oh, Calum!' Tara got up and hugged him hard. Damn Richard and damn Melissa. From now on it was just them who mattered. Her and Calum. There and then she decided to reduce her working hours. Richard would have to subsidise the drop in income. He more than had the means and he more than had the duty to support them. Roll on that court hearing date. 'There's going to be a few changes,' she whispered soothingly, stroking his hair. 'I'm going to be here for you, Calum. I promise.'

Chapter 28

'Careful, easy does it,' whispered Robin to himself as he gently eased the first twin baby out of the car, then passed him to a waiting Jasmine. He followed her while carrying the second sleeping babe, who was totally oblivious to her very anxious but excited and proud parents.

Jemima and Barny had made excellent progress and had been released from their incubators a few days ago. The consultant had declared the babies well enough to be discharged from hospital. Both Robin and Jasmine had been at their side, ritually praying and willing the twins to grow and develop into stronger babies which would allow them to come home. And their prayers had been answered. That day had come.

It was now mid-August and the distant fragrance of heather and chamomile came from the coastline. Yellow flowers of gorse scattered the cliffs and pretty pink blooms of thrift clung to rocks, creeping further inland to join the spiney leaves and blue flowers of sea-holly popping from sand dunes. The sun shone cheerfully in a cloudless, powder blue sky.

'What a beautiful day to bring them home,' remarked Jasmine in a hushed voice, not wanting to wake them.

'It was always going to be a beautiful day, wasn't it?' replied Robin, gazing affectionately at his son and daughter. He unlocked the front door and was just about to push it open when Bunty literally ran up the path to greet them.

'Oh, you've brought them home!' she gushed, stirring the sleeping babies.

Jemima opened her eyes to see Bunty's face staring directly at her and wailed loudly, which in turn set Barny off when she peered down at him too. Jasmine and Robin exchanged a despairing look. So much for not wanting to disturb them.

'My, my, they've both got a good pair of lungs, haven't they?' laughed Bunty, totally ignorant to her unwanted disruption.

'Yes, they have,' replied Jasmine wearily. She was tired and just wanted to get them inside. Robin tactfully intervened.

'Give us a couple of days to get them settled and you're welcome to visit,' he said with a smile.

This seemed to do the trick. Bunty looked from one to the other. The penny dropped.

'Yes, yes, of course. I'll let you get on.' She had one last peek at the twins, then discreetly left them.

'I hope she hasn't taken offence,' sighed Jasmine once they were inside.

'I'm sure she understands,' assured Robin.

It did make them wary though, as to how intrusive their next-door neighbour may be.

'It's only natural that she'd be excited to meet them,' he added.

'I know, but for now it's just you and me. It's our first day home, together as a family,' replied Jasmine.

'It certainly is,' he agreed.

They carefully carried Jemima and Barny upstairs to their nursery. Then after rocking them tenderly back to sleep, placed each one side by side into the waiting cots.

—

'Everything all right, sweetheart?' asked Perry when seeing Bunty return so soon.

'Yes, didn't want to keep them. First day home and all that,' she answered.

'Probably best,' agreed Perry. Then took in her expression. She looked a tad pensive.

He knew how much Bunty was desperate to see the twins and hoped she wasn't hurt at her obvious dismissal. He'd had reservations when she'd seen Robin's car pull up and then get the babies out with Jasmine; but she hadn't given him chance to say anything before dashing out of the house. 'I'm sure there'll be plenty of time to visit.' He patted her shoulder.

'There will,' she agreed.

'Anyway, I've been thinking,' Perry said, quickly changing the subject. This got her attention.

'About what?' she asked.

'A mini-break?'

'Really?'

'Why not? I was thinking of another trip on the boat,' replied Perry.

At this Bunty smiled warmly. 'Oh, that would be lovely.'

That's better, he thought. He didn't like to see his wife quiet and reflective, much better to have her animated and full of life.

'Where to?' she said eagerly.

171

'Thought we could start at Skipton, otherwise known as the gateway to the Yorkshire Dales!' he exclaimed jauntily.

'Ooh, that sounds super!' cried Bunty.

'Good. That's decided then. We'll set off tomorrow,' replied Perry assertively. At least that gives Robin and Jasmine a bit of breathing space, he wisely concluded.

—

The following day saw Bunty and Perry trundle down the garden path, heaving two packed suitcases and a picnic hamper to take to their canal boat. Jasmine, who was at the kitchen sink sterilising baby bottles, noticed the pair through the window and decided to quickly catch them.

'Hi!' she called.

'Off on a canal holiday,' explained Perry with a big beam.

'Lovely! Where to?' asked Jasmine.

'Skipton, Gateway to the Yorkshire Dales,' quoted Bunty with a grin. Then asked, 'How are the twins? Nicely settling in?'

'Yes thanks. We've named them, by the way,' she said. A smile stretched across her face as she took in Bunty's sharp look of anticipation. 'Jemima and Barny.'

'Oh, what beautiful names!' whimpered Bunty.

Perry nodded in approval. 'Yes, great choice.'

'When you get back, you must come for dinner, meet them properly,' invited Jasmine.

'That would be wonderful,' replied Bunty, eyes filling with emotion. Jemima and Barny, her new little neighbours, bless them.

Despite Jasmine and Robin's wish to have a couple of days to themselves, grandparents had other ideas. Of course they did. Both sets of parents simply couldn't keep away. It was inevitable, especially as the twins were the first grandchildren on both sides of the family.

'They're *adorable*!' cooed Jasmine's mum, eager to hold them.

'Steady on, Sue,' warned her father, stopping his wife midway. 'One at a time,' he told her.

They both sat on the sofa holding a grandchild each.

'Take our first photo, Jasmine,' instructed her mum elatedly.

'Already have,' she laughed. 'I've captured your reaction at seeing them.'

'Well done, love,' chuckled Jasmine's dad.

They liked the names chosen for the twins too.

'Barny?' questioned Jasmine's mum, narrowing her eyes in thought, mulling it over.

'It's short for Barnaby, after the surgeon who delivered them,' explained Robin.

'Ah, I see,' she replied.

'Nice gesture,' chipped in Jasmine's dad. He, like the rest of the family, felt a huge debt of gratitude towards all the hospital staff.

'Open the box,' Jasmine's mum told her, tipping her head towards the present they'd brought with them.

Jasmine did so and pulled out two nursery mobiles. One had blue teddy bears suspended from it, the other pink ones. They had a wind-up disc that played 'The Teddy Bears' Picnic'.

'Oh, how wonderful!' exclaimed Jasmine, looking at Robin.

'Thanks, guys,' he said with a wide smile.

'Let's put them up,' suggested Jasmine's dad.

Once Jasmine and her mum were left alone, Sue broached the question which she'd been keen to ask.

'So, you'll be packing in work, won't you, Jasmine?' She'd been concerned at how tired her daughter appeared.

'For the time being,' she conceded. After a few sleepless nights and hectic days, the last thing on Jasmine's mind was graphic design at the moment. Although she did have a few creative ideas drifting through, mainly pictures for the nursery.

'Good.' Her mum nodded, thankful that Jasmine wasn't attempting to push herself. 'And when will Robin go back to work?'

'Not for a couple of weeks. Then I'm going to have to learn to cope on my own.' Immediately she regretted saying those words, as they prompted her mum's next question.

'I can always stay and help?'

'No, it's OK, Mum. Really, I'm sure it'll be fine,' Jasmine hastily assured. After a few minutes they were interrupted by Robin and her dad.

'All set up,' he said, rubbing his hands together.

'I think it's time for their feed,' Robin announced, seeing the babies getting restless.

'It is,' agreed Jasmine, getting up to warm the baby bottles in the kitchen.

'We better get going, love,' said Jasmine's dad.

'Oh, but—'

'No, Sue, we need to leave them in peace,' he gently insisted, much to Robin's relief.

'We'll be back soon,' promised Jasmine's mum with a smile.

Chapter 29

Tara lay in bed, thoroughly enjoying a much-deserved lie in. It was Sunday morning and normally she'd be up early, either dropping Calum off for football practice or catching up with housework. But not today. Calum was at his dad's this weekend, after much coaxing on Richard's behalf, and, in tune with her new outlook on life, Tara had decided to ditch the cleaning. In fact, she thought stretching languidly beneath the bedsheets, she wasn't going to clean ever again. Why should her spare time be spent doing chores, when she worked very hard all week? Actually, working full time was very shortly about to change too. Tara had notified the hospital that she intended to reduce her hours. And now, Tara had also decided to employ a cleaner, someone to come in for a few hours a week and keep on top of the place – and do the ironing. She hated ironing. All this was going to come at a cost, of course, but that didn't worry her judging by the way things were going with Richard.

The notice he had received from the court regarding their hearing date had already proved fruitful. Obviously the details outlining what Tara was applying for had well and truly put the frighteners on him. So much so he had voluntarily upped the maintenance. Well, that was a start, she'd thought with contempt, but if it was merely a ploy to try and stop her going for more and halting the court proceedings, he was badly mistaken. Tara had chosen to stay quiet for the moment when Richard came to collect Calum. The anxious, hopeful look on his face made her stomach turn. Yes, she'd take the increase in maintenance, but that alone was not nearly enough. And they both knew it. She refused to discuss such matters with him in front of Calum so had remained tight-lipped. All the while, Claire was peddling away in the background, seeking financial information regarding Richard's income and the dental practice. By law, he had to comply with the requests being made in preparation for the court hearing, once all the facts and figures had been collated.

Basically, Richard was sweating. He knew the net was closing in and the fear inside him was steadily on the rise. Topping it all, he was taking desperate measures to try and conceal all this from Melissa, who was spending his money like it was going out of fashion. She was also growing bigger by the minute. A jolt of panic shot through him at one point – what if she was having more than one baby? She certainly looked more advanced in her pregnancy. Terror gripped him. How on earth was he going to afford it all? And, to add insult to injury, all the worry was taking its toll. He'd noticed a few more grey hairs, a few more wrinkles and that pouch he'd once been able to keep at bay was making a comeback with all the junk food he'd binged on in anxiety.

So, all in all, things weren't too good for poor, old Richard at the moment. This in itself gave Tara a boost. A part of her took pleasure in seeing the state he was in. He deserved it. But another part of her remained a tad cautious. She knew how ruthless he could be. Look what he'd done after all. No matter how many times Claire had assured her that Richard *had* to conform, Tara didn't have to think too long about how manipulative and cunning her ex-husband was. He was also a bully and used his presence to intimidate her. It was all well and good facing him in a courtroom, but on her own when there was no one else around? She wouldn't put it past Richard to use underhand tactics. In a nutshell, she was wary of him; but not enough to stop what she had started. This time she'd see it through, right to the bitter end. Not just for her, but for Calum too.

If she had a partner, Tara knew full well that Richard wouldn't attempt to pester her, because he was a coward. She'd seen the way he had glared at Jack when he'd brought Calum safely home that evening. Richard wouldn't confront a man up front, he'd just try to make her life a misery instead. For after everything he'd done, he still outrageously believed that Tara was still his, a case of 'nobody else can have her'. Tara was also aware of the way he had used Calum as a pawn too, knowing she was eager to shield him from as much contention as possible. Only now, Calum was making his own mind up, he had views and opinions, which he wasn't scared of sharing. He was also growing up physically too, being as tall as Richard and able to look him in the eye. He wasn't 'little Cal' any more, but a young man who saw his dad for what he was.

Her phone rang on the bedside table. She smiled at seeing Jack's name.

'Morning, gorgeous. Got anything planned today?'

'Morning, Jack,' she said with a laugh. 'Not really.'

'Then let's go out.'

'Sure, why not. Where?'

'Hmm, my surprise. I'll pick you up in an hour.'

'Oh, right…' Tara replied, a touch perplexed.

'Be ready, bye!' And off he went, leaving her with another smile.

On time, Jack arrived exactly an hour later in his sporty little number with the roof down.

'Hop in,' he grinned. He was wearing shades and his blond hair looked windswept. Tara took in his tanned, muscular arms in the white T-shirt he wore. She had pondered over her outfit, not knowing where they were going, but decided in the end for fitted jeans and a smart shirt.

It was a lovely, sunny day and the breeze was refreshing as they drove off.

'So, where are we going, Jack?'

'Somewhere exciting,' he said, raising an eyebrow.

'Where?' She laughed, curiosity setting in.

'Well...' He looked sideways at her before turning back to face the road. 'I thought you deserved a ride on The Big One,' he smirked.

'Pardon?' giggled Tara, then the penny dropped. 'Are we going to the Pleasure Beach?'

He nodded. 'Absolutely.'

'*Jack*!' she squealed in delight. She loved the rides there, being a thrill-seeker. What a spontaneous surprise! When was the last time she'd had one of those? Jack was a breath of fresh air. Then a thought suddenly struck her. What time would they be back? Richard would be dropping Calum off in the evening. Her expression must have changed with her thoughts.

'What's up?' asked Jack.

'What time will we be back? Just thinking of Calum coming home.'

Jack shrugged. 'See if he wants to come.'

'But he's at Richard's,' Tara replied.

'So, text him, see if he'd like to come with us,' Jack said, genuinely not seeing it as a problem.

'I will,' she said firmly. Why shouldn't she? It's not as if Richard hadn't rearranged things with her last minute.

Within a few minutes, Calum sent a reply:

> Deffo!

Tara smiled reading the text.

'He wants to come with us, Jack.' She turned to face him, beaming.

'Good,' he replied with a wink.

Jack had been desperate to cheer Tara up. Knowing how much the court hearing date played on her mind, he was keen to distract her. What she needed was some *fun*, and he was the person to supply it. Once the court proceedings were over and she wasn't so stressed, then he'd ask the questions burning inside him. Until then, he'd do his best to make sure Tara was as happy as possible.

Neither of them could deny the satisfaction they felt at seeing Calum bounce cheerfully out of Richard's house. Nor at the venomous glare Richard gave them.

'Hi, Jack,' said Calum, eyes lighting up at the sporty car with the roof down.

'Hiya, mate, how's it going?' replied Jack, before starting up the engine with a defiant rev (purely for Richard's benefit). They sped off, leaving him furious at the doorway.

The day had been a resounding success. True to his word, Jack had supplied endless fun. He had them laughing all the way to the Pleasure Beach, singing along to the tunes in his car. Calum had been impressed with his choice of music, dubbing him 'cool' once again.

Tara hadn't enjoyed herself so much in a long, long time. It was a most welcome change, being able to relax and really let herself go. Having such a demanding job, not to mention domestic life, made her appreciate the effort Jack had made, not just for her but for Calum too.

After a truly fun-packed day, when they had squealed at the rides, spun on the waltzers, ridden the dodgems and eaten doughnuts, it was time to go home. Calum was practically asleep on the back seat as they drove back to Samphire Bay. A deep orange-pink sun was slowly starting to set by the time they arrived at Augusta House. Jack pulled into the car park and turned to face Tara.

'Thanks, Jack,' she said looking into his eyes.

'My pleasure,' he smiled.

'No, really, thank you so much. Calum's loved it today, so have I.'

They both turned to look at him sleeping peacefully now, then faced each other again. Instinctively their lips met for a gentle kiss, which soon progressed into a passionate one. Tara reached forward as Jack pulled her further into his arms. He felt an overwhelming urge to protect her. Tara's heart was pounding, having not experienced such a gut reaction before. Their actions were visceral, a primeval force to touch each other. They were interrupted by Calum, who was beginning to wake, and parted.

'Mum? Where... Oh...' He rubbed his eyes, fully roused now.

'Back now, buddy,' said Jack with a smile.

'Thanks, again,' said Tara and got out of the car somewhat shakily, still alarmed at the way her body had responded to Jack. Calum joined her and they waved him off.

All the way home, Jack couldn't help the fixed grin that refused to disappear.

Chapter 30

Bunty stood on the deck breathing in the fresh air while Perry steered the boat.

'Ah, doesn't half lift the spirits!' she exclaimed, taking in the canal-side scenery.

'It does. You can't beat a good trip on *The Merry Perry*. It's good for the soul,' agreed Perry. He missed taking himself off on his boat, having previously lived in it. The nomadic lifestyle had suited him well when he'd been single. He admitted it wasn't ideal for everybody though, and certainly saw the advantages of living in a cottage now that he was getting older.

Perry had been pleased with the way Bunty had taken to the narrowboat, like a duck to water, however only in small doses. It was pretty strenuous handling the locks and just jumping on and off onto dry land could be tiring. Not to mention having to stop and refuel or replenish the water tank. And as for emptying the cassette toilet, well, that was well and truly *his* job! But once all the chores were complete and they could relax, chugging along the peaceful waterways was heaven.

After a few hours, they pulled into a mooring point on Skipton marina and tied the boat up to a post.

'Where shall we go first?' asked Bunty with gusto.

That's what Perry loved about her, the way she threw herself into things, lock, stock and barrel. She may be getting older, but was still very much young at heart. They both were. He cast his mind back to years ago, when they were in their early twenties, and not a lot had changed. Bunty was still as beautiful to him now as she was then.

'How about the castle?' he suggested, smiling affectionately at her.

'Good idea!'

After calling for a coffee first, they headed in the direction of Skipton Castle. They climbed up the slope and through the grand gated entrance where they were met by a tour guide, who informed them that, 'Skipton Castle is one of the most complete and well-preserved castles in England.' They were guided through its stone walls holding memories of the past, from medieval times to the civil war. They viewed the banqueting hall, kitchens, bedchambers and privies; climbed from the depths of the dungeon to the top storey of the watchtower.

'It's tiring work, this,' puffed Perry. It made narrowboat life seem easy work.

'I know,' replied Bunty, whose feet were aching.

After the castle tour they went for a well-deserved sit down and lunch.

'Oh, look, the church has a tearoom,' said Bunty, pointing to a sign in the churchyard. 'Let's try it.'

'Very quaint,' remarked Perry as they entered the hall. A piano was playing, and good ladies of the parish attended on red gingham-clothed tables.

'Isn't it?' cooed Bunty with glee, glad of the find. She was even more pleased upon seeing the display of homemade cakes, as was Perry.

'Your usual?' he asked with a grin, spotting the coffee and walnut creation.

Bunty nodded. 'Absolutely. Let's have a sandwich first though.'

'Tuna mayonnaise?' he replied, reading her like a book.

'Right again,' she laughed.

Bunty sat back and watched Perry order the food, sharing banter with the ladies behind the counter. He still had it, she thought fondly. Today he was wearing his favourite paisley waistcoat and jaunty neckerchief. She admired his thick grey hair and the way he moved so fluidly; no bent back or creaking knees with him. Perry Scholar was very much still in his prime she concluded.

Later, they mulled amongst the market stalls on the high street and finished up at the Town Hall. A programme of events was advertised at the entrance, showing the performances it hosted.

'Oh, look, there's a play on tonight,' said Bunty, pointing to the poster. It was some kind of spoof detective drama, judging by the picture depicting a couple of actors. One was wearing a deerstalker hat and smoking a pipe, the other holding a china cup and saucer, waving a biscuit. It was entitled *Who Dunk it?*

'Let's go,' chuckled Perry, immediately relating with the slapstick humour it promised.

'Let's!' gushed Bunty.

As they walked back to the marina they passed several artisan shops; from locally made wicker baskets to cast iron wood burners, the place sold many unique, handcrafted wares. Bunty couldn't resist stopping at a toy shop.

'We must buy something for the twins,' she said, directing them inside.

They were spoilt for choice. It was an Aladdin's cave of every toy imaginable. In the end, Bunty plumped for a soft Peter Rabbit and Flopsy Bunny.

In the evening they decided to have a late supper after the play.

'It's obviously popular,' remarked Bunty as she and Perry entered the Town Hall along with the gathering crowd. They were quietly ushered to their seats and waited with bated breath for the performance to commence.

As Perry suspected, the play was a huge success, with the gut-busting, relentlessly funny two-hander that the audience loved. Bunty couldn't stop giggling all the way through it. After a rapturous applause from the theatre, they trundled out onto the high street again.

'Where do you fancy eating?' asked Perry, glancing across the road at the many eateries.

'Italian?' replied Bunty, noticing a rather charming restaurant lit up invitingly on the corner.

'The Italian Bistro. That looks cosy.' They crossed the road to enter it.

After pizza and a bottle of wine, they decided to call a taxi to drive them back to the marina. It was getting dark and they didn't fancy the walk back. It had been a lovely, eventful day, but they were now tired and in need of a sleep. Their floating bedchamber was calling.

Bunty made them cocoa before snuggling into bed. As night fell, a calmness surrounded the still water of the canal, while all the boats gently rocked their occupants into a deep slumber.

—

Tara was not sleeping well. The following day would bring the court hearing. Her mind spun with every scenario imaginable. What would the District Judge decide? How would Richard react? Anxiety was starting to build, making her chest tighten. She knew the stress symptoms well, having suffered with them for some time, thanks to her ex-husband.

Forcing herself to take deep, steady breaths, Tara willed her body to regulate naturally. God help her at the hearing if she was in this state now, she thought with dread. Then she remembered Claire's words of assurance, telling her she was by her side, fighting her corner. Of course she was – and nobody better than Claire to do so. If anyone was capable of representing her and gaining what she was owed, it had to be the best friend who knew every trick in the book and loophole Richard may contrive. Why had she not listened to her in the first place? Because she'd been too weak and weary, that's why. Not any more. Although wary of the repercussions, Tara was absolutely staunch in her quest to seek what was rightfully hers and Calum's.

She had Jack as moral support too. It was a comfort to know he'd be there and she didn't have to arrive at court alone. In fact, Jack had offered to drive and promised her lunch afterwards, in an attempt to make the day less daunting.

Thinking about Jack helped calm her down. He was proving to be a real rock. He was also bonding with Calum, which she had mixed feelings over. Whilst glad the two liked each other, it also worried Tara that Calum may become too attached. What if it all went disastrously wrong? But, alternatively, what was she supposed to do? Never see anyone and live like a nun?

Thinking about moral support, she wondered if Richard would be coming to court with Melissa, or if he was going to show up solo. Tara was actually beginning to doubt if Melissa even knew about the court case. She wouldn't put it past him to keep shtum in the vain hope of sorting it all out quietly without her knowledge. He was a fool if so, because if Claire managed to get what they were applying for, Melissa would most definitely have to be put in the picture. It would mean a change in her and Richard's lifestyle for sure.

She looked at the bedside clock. It was well past midnight. Sighing, she rolled over and closed her eyes, desperate to get some sleep.

Chapter 31

Jack approached the entrance to Augusta House, wound down the car window and pressed the intercom.

'Come through, Jack.' Tara had been ready, watching for his car to arrive. Calum had got off nicely to school, totally oblivious to what lay in store for his parents in court that day.

She made her way to the car looking very demure in a navy-blue dress and jacket. It was the most formal Jack had seen her.

'Hi, all set?' he asked as she climbed in next to him.

'As well as I'll ever be,' replied Tara in a serious tone. She'd just be glad when the whole thing was over.

'Does Calum know about the hearing?' said Jack, wondering how this was affecting him.

'No. I've kept it from him and it looks like Richard has too.' She turned to face him. 'I don't even think he's told Melissa.'

Jack blinked. 'Really?'

'Yeah, I'm convinced he still thinks he can worm his way out of this, without her knowledge.'

He gave a harsh laugh. 'Then she could be in for a shock.'

'She will if I get what I've applied for,' answered Tara flatly. Not that it bothered her what Melissa thought. It was more the consequences from Richard. She knew full well what to expect from him when he didn't get his own way.

'On a lighter note, I've booked lunch at The Seaview.' Jack smiled, trying his best to keep her upbeat. It worked. Her face broke into a warm beam.

'Oh, thanks, Jack, that'll be lovely.' Then she added, 'Let's hope we've something to celebrate.'

The journey to the County Court didn't take long. They parked up and met Claire, who was waiting in the reception area. If Jack thought Tara looked demure, this was nothing compared to Claire. She wore a tailored black trouser suit with shoulder pads. Pure power dressing. She carried a briefcase, no doubt containing all the facts and figures to throw at Richard. He smiled to himself, already liking her.

'You OK?' Claire searched Tara's face, as if willing her to stay strong.

'Yes,' she nodded. 'Claire, this is Jack. Jack, meet Claire, my best mate.'

'And solicitor,' chipped in Claire with a grin as she shook Jack's hand. She'd been delighted when Tara had previously told her about him and to expect him there.

Jack smiled in return. 'Pleased to meet you.'

'Is he here?' Tara spoke in a hushed voice, eyes darting around the reception area.

'Oh yes,' replied Claire with sarcasm. 'He's already given me a dirty look.'

'Where is he?' asked Jack, frowning. He'd discreetly scanned the area but hadn't seen any sign of him.

'Over there, in a syndicate room with his solicitor.' Claire tipped her head towards a small corridor with three doors.

'He's got representation?' hissed Tara.

'Apparently. A last-minute job. Don't worry, nothing I can't handle,' assured Claire.

Jack believed her. This solicitor friend of Tara's looked the epitome of cool, calm and collected.

Claire checked her watch. 'We're first on the list so won't be delayed.'

Jack questioned if she'd sorted that too. He wouldn't be surprised. She looked completely in control, in her natural habitat, whereas Tara appeared the opposite – nervy and uncomfortable. Yet he knew her inner strength, having witnessed her performance with Jasmine's labour and on the A&E wards. Tara had backbone. She only needed to believe in herself.

Then out came Richard, accompanied by his solicitor, an arrogant-looking middle-aged man, wearing half-rimmed glasses and a haughty expression. Claire gave him a sweeping look and turned to Tara.

'Don't be misled. He may look the part, but he's thick as pig muck,' she whispered with a wink, making Tara and Jack giggle.

'O'Hara and Totty,' announced the court usher.

Tara and Jack exchanged a look.

'You'll be fine,' he said and kissed her cheek.

Richard clocked it and glared at Jack. Jack glared back. Claire noticed the interaction and smirked to herself.

Jack waited in the seating area outside the District Judge's chambers. He watched as Tara held her head high and marched in with Claire. He only hoped it would go well for her. She so deserved it. Once again he was reminded of how intense his feelings for her were. In such a relatively short time he'd developed a strong attachment to her, and the outcome of today was a big deal to him too. He wanted Tara to be happy. He wanted justice for her.

Inside the chambers, Claire was outlining her application.

'Judge, my client is applying for a lump sum, half the current value of her ex-husband's dental practice, given that the business was established with half her money. Indeed, whilst Mr Totty was ploughing the profits made back into the business, the family were living solely on my client's wages. Notwithstanding, Ms O'Hara has been forced to sell the family home, uproot herself and son to a more modest dwelling and continues working full time as a doctor.'

Tara bit her lip. Claire hadn't mentioned the intention to reduce her hours. But then it hadn't been implemented yet, so didn't expect any comeback. She glanced towards Richard who was looking ashen-faced by now. He gulped and straightened his tie. Claire's opening words were met with direct opposition.

'Judge, my client has provided more than generous maintenance and is even prepared to increase it, given reasonable terms.'

Reasonable terms! What an absolute joke, thought Tara, sharply turning to see Claire's response.

'It's because of your client's *un*reasonable terms that we find ourselves here in the first place,' retorted Claire in a steely voice, making Richard wince.

Claire then went on to outline just what little Richard had provided, in comparison to his very lucrative earnings. He at least had the grace to blush.

When hearing it out loud, Tara felt like crying. *How* had she ever agreed to such a pittance? She stole another glance at him. The coward couldn't look her in the eye. It only got worse for him, especially when Claire went on to list the skiing holidays and cruises he and his new wife regularly enjoyed, not to mention the huge house they lived in.

It all made for a deafening, excruciating silence when Claire finished. Tara waited for Richard's solicitor to counteract, but when he finally got his act together and attempted, he blustered profusely, not having any concrete objection. He was finally interrupted by the District Judge.

'I've heard enough. Having perused the file earlier, I have sufficient financial information to make an order in full and final settlement. I grant Ms O'Hara's application, which must be adhered to within three months from the date of this order.'

Basically, as Claire explained once out of chambers, 'Richard has got three months from today to cough up.'

Tara exhaled and closed her eyes. It was over. She'd won.

'Well done.' Jack nudged her arm and smiled.

'I… can't believe it,' she replied in a daze.

'Well, do. It's finally payback time,' said Claire with utter glee, resisting the urge to punch the air.

Richard vanished pretty rapidly, all his nightmares having come true. He'd have to say goodbye to his new home (or at least remortgage it). There'd be no more lavish holidays… And could he really keep his Mercedes Maybach under the circumstances? Doubtful, especially as he'd soon have another child to keep too. Oh, how the mighty crumble, said a taunting voice in his head, or was it his guilty conscience? But what bothered him the most was, how the hell was he going to break the news to Melissa?

'Cheers.' Jack clinked his champagne flute against Tara's.

'Cheers,' she said and took a gulp of fizz. It tasted good. Very good. But then victory always did, didn't it? She sat back in contentment and gave a huge sigh of relief. At last, she was able to relax and no longer had to worry. With the money coming her way, she could easily work part-time and still live comfortably.

When she told Jack what she'd been awarded with, his eyes had widened, not quite believing what Claire had pulled off. 'It's only what's fair,' she'd said, 'and obviously the District Judge thought so too.'

Tara had fully expected a barrage of abusive texts or threatening voice messages, but no, there'd been nothing. Zilch. Richard was silent, for now. This only strengthened her suspicions that he had too much to deal with than contact her. He had a young wife who was soon going to endure a change in lifestyle. Richard was no longer quite the sugar daddy he once was.

Tara turned to face Jack and smiled appreciatively. 'Thanks for your support… and this.' Her hands spread out to the exquisite dining area of the restaurant. It had dark-blue panelled walls, matching the sea that could be seen through the picture window. Hanging lanterns gave the place a warm, mellow glow and the sound of smooth jazz played in the background. The Seaview was renowned for its Michelin Star food and Jack had done well to reserve a table at such short notice.

'My pleasure.' He inclined his head and Tara met his lips with a kiss. 'What time do you have to be back?' he asked in her ear.

Tara gave a sly grin. What was he implying? The champagne filled her senses, giving her a laissez-faire feeling, along with the success in court. 'By four,' she replied.

'Ah, plenty of time.'

'For what?' she asked playfully, looking up at his face.

He returned her gaze, unflinching and gave a lazy smile.

'Coffee, at mine?' He raised a seductive eyebrow.

'Sounds good.' She gave a sexy chuckle.

Chapter 32

Since he was driving, Jack had only drunk one glass of champagne. Nevertheless, his spirits soared as they travelled back to his house.

Tara sat back in the passenger seat in total contentment. Her mood too was lifted. The day had gone better than she could've wished for and it only promised to get better...

She stole a sideways glance at Jack. Hell, he really was handsome. His smoky-grey eyes concentrated on the road ahead, whilst his tanned, muscular arms handled the sports car easily. He had a confident aura, not in an arrogant way, more self-assured, comfortable to just be himself. There were no pretences, hidden agendas or silly mind games, which she'd grown accustomed to in the past. With Jack, what you saw was what you got. And she liked what she saw.

As they approached Samphire Bay, a crackling, sensual tension sizzled between them, each knowing full well how the afternoon was about to pan out. For Jack, it was a moment he'd long waited for and the suspense nearly killed him. For Tara, she'd welcome the warm, soothing sensation of skin on skin, the closeness and comfort it brought. It had been so long since she'd had that kind of pleasure, but she was ready to share it with Jack. He made her feel safe.

Jack turned onto the coastal path leading to his house and noticed in the distance a car parked on the driveway. His heart dropped when realising it was his mother. Bloody hell, of all the timing.

'We've company,' he stated dully.

Tara looked surprised. 'Who?'

'My mother,' he replied in a flat tone.

She didn't quite know how to react. Obviously she was disappointed not to have Jack to herself, but not wanting to appear rude, simply answered, 'Oh, right.'

'Hopefully I'll be able to, you know, wrap things up quickly with her,' he said, knowing it was unlikely. There'd be no chance of his mum going anywhere, not when a new girl was on the scene. Then a dark thought suddenly struck him. What if his dad was with her? He looked at Tara contemplatively and hoped he wasn't. The last thing he wanted was any awkwardness at this stage. There was a time and place for that matter, and this definitely wasn't it. Getting out of the car, he thanked God his mum was alone.

'Darling! I was just about to drive off when I noticed your car on the coastal path,' called his mum.

Great, thought Jack, excellent. A few more minutes would have seen him clear.

'So, you must be Tara.' Jack's mother beamed as she held out a hand.

'Lovely to meet you,' smiled Tara with a handshake.

'This is an unexpected visit, Mum,' said Jack with a wry grin.

'Nonsense!' she scolded. 'Anyone would think I hardly came to visit.' She looked at Tara and rolled her eyes.

They followed Jack up the wooden steps to the door and inside. Jack's frustration rose when his mum headed straight to the kitchen to put the kettle on. She was clearly in for the long haul. He exchanged a look with Tara.

'Sorry,' he mouthed.

Tara grinned back. Evidently the afternoon wasn't going to go quite as planned. Oh well, never mind. There'd be other times; judging by the desire in Jack's eyes, she didn't doubt it.

'So, Tara, come and tell me all about yourself,' said Jack's mum, patting a stool at the kitchen island next to her.

'*Mum*,' cut in Jack with embarrassment.

Tara laughed and sat down as instructed. 'Not a lot to say really. I'm a doctor, a divorcee and have a son called Calum.'

'Not a lot to say!' she exclaimed, knowing Tara's input with Robin and Jasmine's twins. 'I've heard all about your heroic help with Jasmine.'

Tara smiled modestly while turning to look at Jack.

'You were a hero, Tara. I've told everyone about you,' he said calmly, holding her gaze steadily.

All this wasn't lost on his mum, whose face lit up with joy. Could this be the one? She saw the admiration in her son's eyes; it was palpable. Then she remembered the reason for her visit.

'I've some wonderful news,' she announced. Not waiting to be asked, she told them straight away. 'Natalie's pregnant!'

'Isn't that Natalie's news?' asked Jack dryly.

'Well, yes, but I'm sure she won't mind me telling you.'

' 'Course not.' Jack chuckled and sent a look of despair to Tara. She cast her eyes downwards, trying not to giggle.

'Anyway, in celebration, I'm cooking a family meal. Next Sunday.'

'Lovely,' replied Jack, still hoping to cut his mother's visit short.

'And Tara, you must come along too,' she gushed.

There was an awkward pause. Tara turned abruptly to Jack, who was looking back at her with interest.

'Oh... I don't know...' began Tara.

'Nonsense! Of course you're invited, isn't she, Jack?'

All eyes turned to him. There was a silent moment, again.

'Yes, of course,' he agreed. What else could he say? And actually, why not? Perhaps now *was* the time for Tara and his dad to meet. Maybe all those questions he'd been burning to ask were about to be answered after all?

Chapter 33

Jasmine stood over the Moses baskets, smiling tenderly at the two sleeping babies. She'd just fed them, whilst Robin was in the kitchen preparing for their visitors. As promised, Bunty and Perry were coming for dinner. Since bringing the twins home, Robin's domestic skills had known no bounds.

'You're actually a decent cook,' Jasmine had remarked.

'Don't sound so surprised. I lived alone for a few years,' laughed Robin. He refrained from telling her that his diet had mainly consisted of ready-made meals from the local shop, or Sunday roasts at his mum's. Still, even he had to admit his cooking had hugely improved, probably because he'd had to pitch in whilst Jasmine was occupied with the babies. Not that he wasn't a hands-on dad, far from it.

Bath time was his favourite time with them. They loved the water as he gently splashed their wriggling little bodies. He pictured teaching them to swim in years to come, all of them enjoying family life on the bay. Robin, like Jasmine, felt blessed to be bringing their children up in such idyllic surroundings. Although they hadn't been born and raised in Samphire Bay, they were so pleased it was now their home and the place where Barny and Jemima would spend their childhood.

There was a gentle knock on the back door. Jasmine went to the kitchen to see Robin welcome in Bunty and Perry.

'Hi, come in.'

'They're fast asleep at the moment,' said Jasmine, giving Bunty a hug. 'How was Skipton?'

'Wonderful, thanks,' smiled Bunty.

'Here's a little something we bought there for the twins,' said Perry, passing the wrapped presents.

'Oh, thanks,' replied Jasmine, deciding to open them when they were awake.

'Hope you like chilli?' asked Robin.

'Lovely,' replied Bunty, then added, 'did you make it, Robin?'

'I did,' he proudly answered.

'Chilli's his signature dish,' teased Jasmine, having had it quite a few times.

'Practise makes perfect,' chipped in Perry with a chuckle.

'Come through, have a look at them.' Jasmine led them into the sitting room, where the twins still slept peacefully.

'Oh!' cried Bunty on the verge of tears, leaning down for a closer look. Robin and Jasmine exchanged a warm smile. 'Aren't you just adorable?' As if answering her, they both opened their eyes and gurgled, their tiny hands thrusting away. 'Aww...' Bunty was taken away at the sight of them.

'Do you want to hold them?' asked Robin.

'I'd love to,' replied Bunty eagerly. She and Perry sat down next to each other, while Robin and Jasmine gently passed them each a baby. Even Perry's eyes began to fill when Jemima's starfish hand closed over his thumb.

'I can't wait to become a granddad,' he told them gruffly.

'Well, I don't doubt you will be, seeing how happy Emma and Felix look,' said Bunty.

'Ah, still loved-up then?' asked Jasmine with a smile.

'Very much so. In fact, I wouldn't be surprised to hear wedding bells in the not-so-distant future,' replied Perry.

Robin shifted uncomfortably. It bothered him that he and Jasmine weren't married. This only made Jasmine laugh when he voiced his concern, but Robin couldn't help the way he felt. Given his way, he'd have married Jasmine when first learning of their pregnancy, but had agreed to put it off, as preferred by Jasmine. But surely it was time now the twins were here? He looked towards her. She was totally oblivious to his unease. Maybe he should just take the bull by the horns and propose – produce a ring she couldn't resist and name the day.

'Let's open the presents,' suggested Jasmine and gave him a parcel, interrupting his thoughts. 'Aw, they're gorgeous!' she exclaimed, lifting up the Peter Rabbit plush toy.

'Thanks,' smiled Robin. He tucked Flopsy Bunny into Jemima's Moses basket. 'Right, well, I'd better check on dinner.'

Once gone, Bunty grinned at Jasmine. 'Robin seems very domesticated.'

'He's brilliant. I don't know how I'll cope when he goes back to work.'

'Well, we're always here to help,' said Perry and sincerely meant it. He'd surprised himself at how the twins had affected him. He gazed down and saw two tiny blue eyes staring back at him and melted.

Meanwhile, Robin was busy in the kitchen. Not only seeing to the food, but his mind had suddenly notched up a gear. A plan was forming and building momentum. He realised that he needed to be far more assertive, especially where Jasmine was concerned. He'd always admired her pragmatic approach, and still did. He applauded her get-on-with-it attitude, especially given her traumatic past. Becoming a widow at the age of twenty-nine and starting again in Samphire Bay couldn't have been easy. Not everyone would have coped the way Jasmine did. She'd shown real resilience and strength of spirit. But, at times, Jasmine could be a little too blasé, too casual. Look at how she'd insisted on going to the launch party, saying she would be 'fine'. Clearly that had been a mistake. He ought to have intervened, put his foot down. And now he was going to show some assertiveness. He was going to insist that they marry and make their union official. Why not, for goodness' sake? They were blissfully happy, had two beautiful children and a lovely home.

'It's ready!' he called, placing the casserole dish filled with chilli on the table along with a big bowl of rice. He'd also made a salad and garlic bread.

'Hmm, this smells delicious,' said Bunty, sitting down.

'It certainly does,' added Perry, rubbing his hands together.

Jasmine moved Barny into Jemima's Moses basket so they could keep each other company while the adults ate. That was the beauty of twins, she thought, they always had each other. She sat at the table and poured the wine, allowing herself just half a glass.

Robin took off his apron and joined them. He raised his glass and gave a toast.

'To us,' he cheered and looked directly at Jasmine. She gave a slight frown before raising her glass, expecting a toast to the twins if anything.

'To us,' they all repeated, clinking glasses.

After a relaxing meal, which the babies didn't interrupt, Bunty and Perry bid their farewells. Under strict instruction from Perry, Bunty was aware of outstaying her welcome.

'We can't stay too long. They'll be tired and want to put the babies to bed,' he'd warned. Bunty had nodded in agreement, glad of the advice. The last thing she wanted was to become a pest.

Once the twins had been bathed and fed again, Jasmine wound up the musical mobiles suspended over the cots. The tune seemed to soothe the babies and settled them down for the night.

'I just need to pop out,' whispered Robin, opening the nursery door.

'Where to?' asked Jasmine in surprise.

He winked. 'All will be revealed.'

'But, Robin—'

'Won't be long,' he interrupted and disappeared, leaving a very puzzled Jasmine.

—

'Grandma's ring?' said Robin's mum, raising an eyebrow.

'Yeah. She left it to you, didn't she?'

'Well, yes, but I was saving it to pass on to a future granddaughter, Jemima now.'

'Can I have it?'

'Pardon?' she laughed.

'I want to give it to Jasmine, tonight. I'm going to propose,' he declared with fortitude.

Good for him, she thought, knowing her mother would have approved. Of course she would.

'I'll fetch it.'

Within minutes she was back with the ring, still in its original box. It would be considered a collectable nowadays. A stunning blue topaz, claw set in a golden band. It matched the blue velvet box with the name of the jewellers in gold writing.

'It'll be in safe hands, that's if she says yes,' said Robin with a grin.

'Of course she will,' reassured his mum.

—

Jasmine was in the sitting room when Robin came back.

'What's going on?' she asked with a frown.

Robin knelt in front of her.

'Jasmine, will you marry me?' Before she could answer, he produced the velvet box. Instinctively, Jasmine took it and opened the lid. She gasped.

'Robin, it's *beautiful*.' Then, realising she hadn't answered him, looked into his eyes. 'Yes, of course.'

Robin placed the ring on her finger.

'A perfect fit,' she said in delight.

'Obviously meant to be,' replied Robin.

They kissed, then Robin pulled back.

'I want to set the date.'

Jasmine paused. 'When?'

'Before the twins are christened.'

Another pause. 'Why not at the same time?' suggested Jasmine.

'What, you mean a wedding and christening together?'

'Well, everyone we know will be there. Why not get the twins christened and exchange vows too?'

Robin blinked. Jasmine took being practical to a new level. It did make sense though. Everyone they knew *would* be there in church, so yes, why not? It's what he wanted, wasn't it? His little family all nicely sorted. His face broke into a beam.

'You're on.'

Chapter 34

It was Sunday, the day of the family meal at Jack's parents' house. He still didn't know how to feel about it. Once his mother had eventually finished her visit, very little time was left for what he and Tara had had planned, more's the pity. It did give him chance though to speak to her about the dinner though.

'You really don't have to come, that is, if you don't want to.' Then realising how that might sound, quickly added, 'What I mean is, don't feel pressured into it.' He'd given a cheerful smile, to show no offence would be taken if she declined the invite. But to his surprise, Tara had merely shrugged.

'I'm fine about it, as long as you are?' She'd eyed him closely, gauging his reaction.

Was she challenging him? They looked each other in the eye. Jack blinked first.

'Of course I am,' he replied. And he was. More than anything, Jack was keen to see how Tara and his dad responded to each other.

One thing for sure, the day promised to be an interesting one, reflected Jack as he headed out of his house to pick Tara up.

Tara had dropped Calum off at his friend's for the day and was due to collect him early evening. She was glad, as it gave her an excuse to leave Jack's parents' should she need one. Whilst not anticipating confrontation of any kind, a part of her was naturally apprehensive. And with good reason. But she could feel herself growing extremely close to Jack now and knew it was inevitable she'd be expected to face his father at some point. A family meal was probably going to be the best scenario, when everyone, including his wife, was there. Austin Knowles definitely wouldn't want to cause a scene, it was in *his* interest not to, not hers. Above all, Tara felt vindicated in her actions. She was not the villain, far from it. She'd simply acted with the best intention.

Tara chose to wear smart but casual clothes. Conscious of not wanting to look like she'd overly made an effort, giving the occasion too much gravitas, she'd plumped for khaki trousers and a cream T-shirt. When Jack arrived, she was glad to see him in just jeans and a T-shirt too. Obviously it wasn't going to be a formal affair.

They drove in a companiable silence, each deep in their thoughts. As expected, Jack's mum gave them a big welcome.

'Lovely to see you again!' she cried, kissing their cheeks. 'We're in the garden. Come and join us.'

Jack and Tara followed her down the hall and through the lounge patio doors.

'Everyone, meet Tara!' she announced with gusto.

Natalie was first up off her deckchair. 'Hi, Tara, I'm Jack's sister, Natalie,' she said, holding her hand out.

'Pleased to meet you, Natalie, and congratulations,' smiled Tara.

'Oh, thanks. Another to add to the brood,' she joked, nodding towards her two boys, who were busy kicking a football with her husband. He waved up at them and shouted over.

'Hi, Tara, I'm Steve!'

'Hi!' called back Tara.

'Where's Dad?' asked Jack, surprised not to see him.

'He's had to pop out,' said his mum, rolling her eyes. 'Something urgent came up at the office.'

Jack frowned. What could be so 'urgent' on a Sunday at the office? His suspicions rose.

'Uncle Jack, come and play!' shouted his nephews.

'Yeah, give me a break,' said Steve, laughing as he came to join them.

Jack smiled at Tara. 'Fancy a kick-about?'

Tara shook her head. 'I don't think so.'

'Of course she doesn't,' scolded his mum, then turned to Tara. 'Go and sit down. I'll get the drinks. Prosecco OK?'

'Oh, lovely, thanks,' replied Tara, feeling the need for alcohol. Soon she was sat next to Natalie sipping a very welcome glass of fizz.

'Jack's told me all about your amazing delivery of Robin's twins,' gushed Natalie.

'*I* didn't deliver them, thank goodness, just rang the air ambulance,' said Tara.

'*Just*? You saved the day,' replied Natalie incredulously. Then she turned at seeing her dad walk through the patio doors into the garden. Tara quickly turned too. Suddenly Jack was next to her.

'Dad, meet Tara,' he said, scrupulously looking for his response. Then his eyes darted towards Tara for hers.

'Pleased to meet you, Tara,' said Austin and nodded his head. He didn't offer her a hand.

'And you,' replied Tara with a tight smile.

Jack's gaze swept back on his dad, and there it was, that tell-tale sign, the nervous tick below his eye. In fact, his dad had broken out in a sweat and appeared to have difficulty breathing. His forehead was covered in perspiration. Slightly alarmed, Jack looked to Tara, who by her expression had noticed. His dad appeared more than uncomfortable – he looked positively ill. Jack's mum was just returning from the kitchen.

'Ah, there you are, Austin. Have you been introduced to Tara?'

There was a slight awkward pause before he answered, 'Yes. We've met.' Then they were interrupted by the boys playing football.

'Granddad, come and play!'

Jack, eager for his dad to sit down, intervened. 'Let Granddad have a rest. He'll play after,' he told them, then directed him towards the deckchairs. 'Sit down, Dad.'

All the time Tara was assessing the situation. She too had clocked Austin's behaviour. He was clearly distressed, judging by the way his face twitched and the droplets of sweat which were pouring from it. His breathing was becoming more laboured too. She instinctively looked towards his left arm. To her horror, she saw him grip it.

'Dad? Are you all right?' asked Natalie in concern.

'I... I...' Austin held his arm and doubled over in pain, then slumped onto the floor. His body lay there, lifeless.

'Austin!' shrieked Jack's mum.

Jack frantically turned to Tara, who instantly bolted to Austin. Within seconds she was knelt at his side, checking for a pulse. She put the heel of her hands in the middle of his chest, interlocking her fingers, making sure they didn't touch his ribs. Keeping her arms straight, she began to press down hard, then allowed the chest to come back up. She kept on pushing, then gave him two rescue breaths by pinching his nose and blowing directly into his mouth.

'Call an ambulance!' yelled Natalie, while Tara valiantly continued with resuscitation.

By the time the ambulance came, Austin was stable and breathing. All thanks to Tara, who once again liaised with the emergency team as they stretchered him into the ambulance and off to hospital. Jack's mum had jumped in the back with him, leaving Jack and Natalie traumatised. Steve was inside with the boys, who had been ushered away out of the commotion. Natalie, in tears, went to join them.

Tara faced Jack, pale and distraught. She went to hug him, but he pushed her away. Expecting it was shock that had made him reject her, she was staggered at his next words.

'Tara, why exactly did you ring my dad?'

She stood, staring at him as the words sunk in. How did he know about her ringing Austin? Surely his dad hadn't told him. They were interrupted by Steve, who'd just come through the patio doors.

'I'm taking Natalie and the boys home,' he said gravely.

Jack turned to him. 'Of course. I'll come and see you off.'

Tara was left alone for a few minutes, giving her time to collect herself. When Jack returned, he faced her again, obviously still waiting for an answer.

'Sit down,' she instructed and walked towards the deck-chairs. Once sat opposite him, she took a deep breath and began. 'A close friend of mine came to me for help. She was in a real state, anxious and... frightened at what she'd done. Basically, she'd been seeing someone behind her husband's back and wanted it to stop. She was petrified her husband was going to find out. When she tried to end the affair, he wouldn't accept it was over. He continued to contact her, on the brink of pestering, until she was a nervous wreck. I advised a prescription of mild tranquilisers to calm her down and offered to speak to the man, explain how he was stressing my friend out and that it was over.' There was a deadly pause.

'And that man was my dad,' stated Jack bleakly.

'Yes, it was,' confirmed Tara in a quiet voice.

So, it was finally out. Could have been worse, reflected Jack. Tara could have been the woman his dad had been seeing. Then another thought struck him. 'Your friend, is she called Sarah?' he asked in a flat voice.

Tara blinked. 'Yes, she is,' came her surprised reply. 'How do you know her name?'

Jack gave a long sigh. 'We knew about the affair. He actually came clean to my mum. It very nearly ruined their marriage, but fortunately they got through it.' He looked up with tears in his eyes. 'But it left an impression on me and Natalie. I've never really forgiven him.'

'I'm sorry, Jack. If it's any consolation your dad was civil on the phone. I think my contacting him as Sarah's friend made him realise how stupid they'd both acted, putting their marriages at risk.'

'Mum and Dad do seem to be much happier now,' conceded Jack, nodding.

Fundamentally, Tara hadn't told him anything he didn't already know, except of course her involvement in all of it.

'How did my dad know it was you? I mean, he hadn't seen you, had he? And yet as soon as I mentioned your name, it clearly resonated with him.'

'I introduced myself as Tara, Sarah's friend. I assume Sarah must have mentioned me, and that I was a doctor.'

It suddenly dawned on Jack, remembering the conversation he'd had with his dad.

'Yes, only when I gave your full name, *Doctor* Tara O'Hara, did he flinch.'

'Well, there you are then,' replied Tara sitting back. She observed Jack's ashen face and wanted to reach out and comfort him, but would he want that now? Their eyes met. 'Does this change things between us, Jack?' she asked evenly.

'No. To be honest, with the scenarios running through my mind, the truth's a blessing.'

Tara frowned.

'I found your number on my dad's phone and, well…'

'Oh, *Jack*,' replied Tara, realising what he must have thought. 'Why didn't you just ask me?' she said incredulously.

'I wanted to, I really did, but it never seemed the right moment. What with all you're going through with Richard, it just… I don't know. It didn't feel appropriate to put you on the spot.'

'I'm only sorry the truth's come out under such circumstances,' Tara replied sadly.

'You saved my dad's life. I can't thank you enough,' gulped Jack.

'The ambulance should have arrived now. I'll ring the hospital and get an update.'

She pulled out her mobile from her pocket and made the call, speaking calmly and efficiently. Jack took it all in, her quiet, measured manner, totally in control. Yet again she'd saved the day. He was completely in awe of her.

Moments later Tara gave the encouraging news that his dad was still stable and that his mum was to spend the night in hospital with him. Jack heaved a huge sigh of relief and text Natalie with the information. There was nothing they could do now, apart from visit them tomorrow.

Chapter 35

Jack entered the hospital, hoping to see his dad still in a stable condition. His mum had rung him to say he'd been transferred to a general ward and out of intensive care earlier on. Much to his relief, Austin was sat up in bed looking settled. His face lit up when seeing Jack approach him.

'Dad, how are you feeling?'

'Tired, but better, thanks.'

Jack sat down beside his bed.

'Where's Mum?' he asked.

'She's gone for a coffee and some fresh air,' replied Austin, then closed his eyes briefly and inhaled deeply. 'Listen, Jack, there are things I need to tell you,' he started, wanting this conversation before his wife returned.

'I know, Dad. Tara's told me everything,' interrupted Jack in a quiet voice. Their eyes met. Jack was shocked to see his dad's were teary.

'I never wanted to hurt your mother. It was a big mistake, which I'll regret for the rest of my life.' Then he gave a harsh laugh. 'Which could easily have ended yesterday, if it wasn't for Tara.' He looked straight into Jack's face.

'I know,' was all he could say and gulped.

'She's a… remarkable woman and I can't thank her enough, despite… you know,' Austin trailed off, not quite knowing the best way to express himself.

'Dad, we have to draw a line under the whole thing. You and Mum, you're OK now, aren't you?'

'Absolutely,' said his dad and nodded firmly. 'The woman's a saint.'

'Yes. She is,' replied Jack resolutely.

'And I'll never hurt her again,' continued Austin, still staring at Jack.

'Good, then let's—'

'Oh, Jack, you're here!' called his mum, scurrying up the ward. She came to give him a hug.

'You OK, Mum?' asked Jack softly.

'*I* am. It's him we're all worried about,' she replied, pointing towards her husband. His head bent downwards, unable to meet her gaze.

Guilty conscience, thought Jack. Good. Hopefully his dad had learnt a lesson, convinced it was his shame and stress that had contributed towards his heart attack. Now he knew Tara was no longer a threat to him, and *he* certainly didn't want any awkwardness between his dad and girlfriend, optimistically, relations should improve between them all. Judging from his dad's words, he was at pains to keep his mum happy, which was precisely what Jack wanted. As long as everyone played their part, his family could be a content one, he felt sure. After all, Tara *did* save his dad's life. They all owed her. And Tara? She was just glad Jack knew the truth about her involvement in it all. Surely they could all put the past behind them?

As if reading his mind, Austin held out his hand. Jack took it.

'Thank Tara for me, won't you?'

'Yes, I will,' he said with a smile.

—

Tara was actually busy in the nearby ward. She'd resisted going to see Austin, knowing his wife was with him, but knew Jack was due to visit that morning. Then, just as she'd been thinking about him, she saw his face through the glass door at the bottom of the ward. He'd obviously wanted to catch her, if possible. Luckily, Tara had just finished with a patient, so quickly walked to the door and opened it.

'How did he look?' she asked with searching eyes.

'OK. He sends his eternal thanks,' replied Jack with a half-smile.

'Good. I'm just glad he's recovered well,' answered Tara.

Jack couldn't have admired her more. His dad was right, she really was remarkable.

'Are you free this evening?' he asked with hope.

'Yes. Richard's got Calum tonight,' replied Tara. 'And I'm off tomorrow,' she added with a twinkle in her eye.

'Are you indeed?' said Jack seductively, raising an eyebrow. Then the moment was lost as her pager bleeped into life.

'Gotta go,' she uttered and rushed off.

What a woman, thought Jack, watching her rush down the ward to the next emergency.

—

Later that day, after a long, hard shift, Tara saw the text from Jack.

> Dinner's at mine. Bring your swimsuit.

Hmm, what did he have in mind? she chuckled to herself, a swim in the sea or a dip in his hot tub? Either way she was looking forward to sinking her tired body into refreshing water. That and a glass of wine. It was great having a couple of extra days off, now her part-time hours had commenced. It was even better knowing Richard's final settlement was due to arrive soon. His solicitors had contacted Claire to say the money would be deposited imminently. So, yes, life was certainly on the up, especially compared to a few months ago, when she'd been exhausted and worried about her finances. Even Calum seemed a little more settled now. Richard, knowing the law was on her side, had to play ball now, and ensure their child arrangements were adhered to. No more playing silly buggers. He'd collected Calum on time and stuck to his routine, which, in turn, made for a more content child.

Calum had mentioned there being an atmosphere at his dad's for a period of time, but all had calmed down now. It seemed Melissa was occupied these days, having returned to work for the time being at the dental surgery. Tara couldn't help but smirk to herself at hearing this. So yes, life was sweet at the moment and long overdue. She collected her jacket, bag and phone, then closed the locker door and set off home to freshen up before heading to Jack's.

Deciding to walk to his house, Tara strolled through the wooded area leading onto the beach, carrying a rucksack. She'd packed a few overnight things, it being a tacit assumption she'd be staying over. It was utterly refreshing walking barefoot once by the shore, feeling the cold waves tingle over her feet. She looked up at the pink evening sky as the sun was slowly starting to set and breathed in the fresh, salty air. This was the life. She couldn't remember feeling such a state of contentment.

As Tara reached The Cove, she saw Jack outside on the decking, stood over a barbeque.

'Hi!' she called, waving. He looked up and smiled. She climbed up the wooden steps to meet him and they kissed.

'Hope you're hungry,' said Jack, turning over the steaks on the grill. It was packed with mushrooms, onion rings, tomatoes and sweetcorn. There were two baked potatoes in tinfoil keeping warm.

'Hmm, smells delicious,' she replied, watering at the mouth. 'Here, I brought this.' She rummaged in her rucksack and pulled out a bottle of wine.

'Ah, lovely, thanks. Fancy pouring us a glass?' He nodded towards the kitchen where the glasses were.

As Tara went inside, she was, as ever, struck by the design and sheer style of the place. It never failed to impress her. She could well see why it had won architectural awards. Reaching for the wine glasses, she noticed a framed picture on the kitchen shelf, one she hadn't seen before. It was a large black-and-white photo of Jack with his sister and father, all laughing, arms round each other, stood in front of his house. Underneath was a written caption: 'The Dream Team'.

How proud they must be, thought Tara with a smile. She poured the wine and took the glasses outside. Handing one to Jack, she remarked on the photograph.

'That's a good picture of you, Natalie and your dad.'

Jack turned whilst still tending to the barbeque.

'Yeah, Mum took it the day I moved in. We had a family party to celebrate.' Then he asked, 'Did you bring your bikini?' with a grin.

'All in the rucksack.' She grinned back, failing to add that she'd actually packed a few overnight things too.

'Good. I've got the hot tub bubbling nicely,' he winked.

'Sounds good,' she chuckled into her wine glass, whilst imagining Jack's body in trunks. Yes, life was *definitely* on the up!

They ate outside on the decking area, overlooking the splendid view of the bay. The sound of lapping waves was therapeutic, making them both relax. As always, Jack had cooked everything to perfection.

'That was absolutely delicious,' sighed Tara, sitting back with satisfaction.

'It's the least I can do,' replied Jack, refilling their glasses with wine.

'Just doing my job,' she shrugged.

'No, Tara. Much more than that,' said Jack, staring into her eyes. They held each other's gaze. No more words were necessary.

As the sun set over the glistening water, the sky grew darker with a sprinkling of stars. Perfect, thought Jack, hoping for such a setting.

'Come on, let's get into the hot tub,' he suggested with glee.

He showed her into his bedroom to change. Tara was once again in awe of his taste, from the bespoke chunky wooden bed, to the en-suite with a walk-in shower. He nipped to the bathroom nearby and was soon ready and waiting outside the bedroom door. Then out she came, making Jack's jaw drop, wearing a russet two-piece costume which covered her body discreetly whilst still showcasing her curves. It was chic and classy, just like the lady herself. Tara, too, was taking in Jack's toned, muscular torso and firm thighs.

'Ready?' he gulped.

'Absolutely,' she smirked.

Chapter 36

Jack woke with a long, lazy and satisfying stretch, then glanced at Tara sleeping peacefully. Hell, she was even more gorgeous asleep. He watched her exquisite body gently rise and fall, one that he'd eagerly explored last night – and she too had got very accustomed with his, he reflected happily whilst chuckling to himself.

Tara stirred and slowly opened her eyes. For a moment she halted, waking to unfamiliar surroundings, then smiled at seeing Jack's face hover over her.

'Sleep well?' He gave a sexy grin.

'Hmm, not bad,' she replied with a low chuckle.

'Breakfast in bed. You stay there,' ordered Jack before kissing her lips.

'Sure?'

'Yeah, just chill. I won't be long,' he said whilst getting up and slipping on his jeans.

As Tara's eyes slid over his tanned, firm body, images of last night flashed into her mind. And what a night it had been, full of urgent passion. Jack's body and hers instinctively moved together, almost as one. They had responded in unison, like long-lost lovers, not like the first encounter it actually was. Tara felt like she'd known Jack all her life, such was the connection between them.

Jack, too, was musing on their lovemaking and couldn't help the wide beam refusing to disappear on his face.

He also hadn't ever felt such a bond. No doubt about it, they were most definitely compatible. He busied himself heating croissants and making coffee, then trayed it up and went back upstairs.

Kicking the bedroom door open, he entered to find Tara stood by the balcony wrapped in a towel. Her hair was wet from the shower. She had her back to him and was admiring the bay.

'I'd never get tired of this view,' she sighed.

'I don't. It changes daily, depending on the weather and time of year,' replied Jack, putting the tray on the bedside table. 'Do you want breakfast out there?'

'That'd be lovely.'

He moved to push the balcony doors open and came back for the tray.

'I better get dressed,' said Tara quickly, collecting her clothes and heading for the bathroom. She put on fresh joggers and a T-shirt, then joined him to sit at the bistro table. Once again her eyes admired his side profile, lit up by the hazy morning sunshine. 'Thank you.' She smiled as he poured her coffee and handed over the croissants. 'This is a treat.'

Jack assessed her relishing her breakfast. He liked a girl who wasn't afraid to show her appetite. He recalled cooking dinner for one or two who'd only pecked at the food he'd made them and had been irritated by it.

'What do you normally have for breakfast?' he asked.

'Hmm.' She wiped her mouth from flakes before answering. 'Not much to be honest. Don't have time. Mornings are rushed, getting Calum off to school and going in to work.'

'But that'll be different now, won't it? With your part-time hours?'

'Yes, it'll be a welcomed change,' she said with a broad smile. It took some getting used to, having more time to herself and Calum… and now Jack. She eyed him over her coffee cup.

'What?' he laughed, sensing her sizing him up.

'How many times have you done this?' she asked, head cocked to one side.

'Eaten breakfast out here? Many times,' he replied glibly.

'No. How many times have you eaten breakfast out here with *a woman*?' she corrected.

'Honestly?' Jack looked at her.

'Yes.' She stared back.

'None. You're the first.'

There was a pause. Whilst not entirely expecting that answer, she was glad of it. But was it the truth? Her eyes narrowed in contemplation. Why would he lie? To make her feel special? She already did. Jack had shown nothing but care and consideration.

'What are you thinking, Tara?' he gently asked, wanting to know what was going on inside that pretty head of hers.

'Nothing.' She shrugged.

'Oh, I think you were,' he laughed softly. 'But let me assure you, *you* are the only lady who's sat out here, enjoying this view, breakfasting with me.'

'I believe you,' she replied, then added with a grin, 'but how many have been in your hot tub?'

'Ah… well…'

They both fell into giggles. Not for one moment did Tara suppose Jack hadn't entertained many a woman in the hot tub. She could only imagine the parties that he must have thrown here. The Cove cried out for them, it was the ideal place. And Jack was a handsome, young, hot-blooded male. End of.

Changing the subject, Jack asked, 'So, what do you fancy doing today?'

Tara breathed in the fresh sea breeze.

'Chilling out here. Fancy a swim in the sea?'

'Sure. I'll pack a picnic.'

Tara loved the slow pace of life that living by the beach dictated. It was such a contrast to what she was used to before moving to Samphire Bay. Although she'd loved city life in Lancaster, it had always been a tad rushed. Sitting in traffic, watching people everywhere going about their business, houses overlooking each other, no privacy. Here, nature was your only neighbour, that and the beautiful, turquoise bay with its golden sandy dunes. Together they walked, hand in hand along the shoreline. Tara had never known peace like it.

At the end of a perfect day, Jack drove her home and kissed her goodbye. Tara had to be back for Calum, who was being dropped off by his dad.

'Thanks for a fabulous time,' she said, opening the car door.

'My pleasure. See you soon.'

She waved him off, then made her way into Augusta House. Entering the apartment, her mood instantly changed. Calum was already back, judging by the music coming from his bedroom, and there on the sofa was Richard.

'What are you doing here?' she rasped.

'And hello to you too, Tara,' came the sarcastic reply. 'Good night?' He arched an accusing eyebrow, then stood up menacingly with an envelope in his hand. 'Thought

I'd hand deliver this.' He gave a tight smile and shoved it in her hand. Then without another word, left.

Tara stared down at the envelope. With a slightly trembling hand, she ripped it open. Her chest started to thump at reading the letter.

Dear Tara,

I decided to put all this in writing, as advised by my solicitor.

I intend to apply for full care and control of Calum. As you stated at the court hearing, or rather Claire did, you've always had an exhausting, stressful career. Perhaps it's time for our son to enjoy being in a less demanding environment, which your job clearly creates.

I consider it in his best interests to be part of a complete family which provides love and care from both his father and stepmother, and of course his future siblings, one of which is due to arrive soon.

So, Tara, you'll be free to enjoy your single life and all that may involve, presumably that young beau you've picked up. Congratulations, for now that is.

My solicitor will be in touch, who, by the way, is not the last one that represented me. Now that I've had time to reflect, I've done my research and paid for the best. I take it you'll still keep good old Claire? Well, whoever, you're going to need a bloody good one, because rest assured, I mean business.

See you in court, again,
Richard

Tara resisted the urge to throw up. Instincts told her Richard was serious. Of course he was. Now that he'd had time to recover and lick his wounds from the last court order made, he was fighting back. She grabbed her phone and rang Claire. She'd know what to do.

Fortunately, Claire answered quite quickly. Once Tara had read out the contents of Richard's letter she snorted with derision.

'Tara, it's bullshit. He's just lashing out. Trying to hurt you,' she retorted. On a more urgent note she asked, 'Has the final settlement come through yet?'

Tara paused. She hadn't checked her bank balance for a couple of days. She'd been busy at work and then at Jack's.

'I don't know...'

'Look now,' insisted Claire.

Tara went to her laptop and logged onto her bank account. It had arrived that morning. She closed her eyes in relief. Thank God.

'Yes, it went in today,' she confirmed to Claire who was waiting with bated breath.

'Right. So he's pissed off and wants revenge. He's using Calum as a pawn,' she replied with disdain.

Fury mounted inside Tara. Well, if it's a fight Richard wanted, he'd bloody well get one. They were interrupted by Calum coming out of his bedroom. Tara quickly ended the call.

'Anything to eat, Mum?' he asked nonchalantly, oblivious to what was going on.

'I'll make us something.' She cleared her throat and tried to sound casual. 'Err... How did Dad get into the car park?'

'He didn't. We parked outside and walked in. I did remember to text, but my mobile was dead. Forgot to charge it. Sorry.'

Tara took a deep breath. It wasn't Calum's fault his dad was crafty by avoiding the Augusta House car park and gaining entry.

She gave her son a false smile. 'Maybe make sure it's charged in future, yeah? It's important, Calum.'

'OK. What's for tea?'

Well, at least it looked like Richard hadn't said anything to their son yet, she thought. But how long would it be before he disrupted their lives again?

Chapter 37

Jasmine and Robin were drawing up a list of invites for their wedding/christening. Now that Robin had got used to the idea of an all-in-one occasion, he'd seen the logic that Jasmine's suggestion held. Of course it made perfect sense when considering it. Why have two separate events when everyone they wanted there would be under the same roof? The church roof, that is. In fact, he'd rather taken to the novelty of it. It would certainly be a day to remember.

Choosing the Godparents had been a no-brainer. Tara was obviously the number one choice for Godmother, and Robin wanted Jack to be the twins' Godfather *and* his best man.

Now they were deciding on the guests. As well as family and friends, many from Samphire Bay would be attending.

'What about Emma and Felix?' asked Jasmine. 'We did get an invite to their TV drama launch party.'

'I think so. We don't want to offend Perry and Bunty in any way,' replied Robin.

'Hmm, that's true. I'm not sure Perry would appreciate us leaving his daughter out.' She hesitated before continuing, 'But do you think Felix would want to come?'

'Why not?' frowned Robin.

'You don't think it would be a bit... provincial for him? Being a famous actor and all?'

'No,' said Robin sounding a touch offended. 'Look how he enjoyed Perry and Bunty's wedding. He loved it.'

'Yeah, but did you notice how *everybody* was looking at him too?' replied Jasmine.

Robin laughed. 'Oh, I get it. You don't want him stealing the bride's thunder?' he teased.

'Or the twins',' retorted Jasmine.

'Don't worry. I'm sure all eyes will be on you.'

'On *us*,' corrected Jasmine.

She still hadn't picked her wedding dress. A part of her wondered if she should just buy a smart suit, but Robin had been appalled by the notion, as had Bunty, when running it past her. She'd shook her head firmly.

'Darling, no. Absolutely not. You are the *bride* and must look radiant in white, not like some kind of business executive!'

Jasmine had rolled her eyes, but did accept her friend's view. She refrained from pointing out to both her and Robin that this was her second time, and that she'd already done 'the big white wedding' thing. It could easily have been taken the wrong way and didn't want to cause any offence. However, Jasmine *did* want her wedding to Robin to be very different to her first one. Clearly it would be with the twins getting christened, but still, she didn't want to have a traditional white wedding dress. It just didn't feel right. Not having the courage to say all this to Robin, Jasmine had kept it to herself, for now. Truth be told, she didn't quite know what to wear. Bunty had been all for a spot of retail therapy, excited to help her choose a dress. She'd envisaged a real girly day out, full of fun and excitement, but Jasmine had feigned tiredness, using the twins as an excuse not to go.

'I'm exhausted at the moment, Bunty. I'll wait till nearer the time,' she'd told her.

Only time was creeping up now and she was still clueless. It hadn't helped when Robin had come back from a successful day's shopping with Jack. The pair of them had bought matching grey morning suits and had looked amazing when trying them on for her.

'Oh, you both look so smart, very dapper!' she'd gushed, and truly meant it.

'Well, it's not every day you're the Godfather *and* best man,' beamed Jack proudly.

Jasmine appreciated the effort people were making, but a stillness lingered inside her. She couldn't put her finger on it. It wasn't doubt, because that was the one thing she'd never had concerning Robin. He was her rock, always had been, and now the father to her children – and a great one at that. No, maybe the feeling she had was merely the comparison to her first wedding. Now that really had been the full works.

It been a white wedding in every sense. Snow had gently floated as she stepped out of the vintage Rolls-Royce, trailing ivory silk and clutching a posy of cream roses. Tom had stood at the alter looking tall and handsome in his charcoal suit (not dissimilar to Robin and Jack's, ironically). After a full church service, they'd swept down the aisle to confetti and applause, out into the snowflakes, to sip champagne in the back of the Roller that took them to the five-star Georgian hotel. There, a magnificent banquet was held, followed by dancing and live music from a band. It had been magical.

Jasmine still thought of Tom, of course she did. After all, he hadn't been long gone – just under two years – but such a lot had happened to her in that time. Occasionally, she'd reflect on the life she'd had in their narrowboat, *Moonshine*, chugging along the canal without a care in the world. Then, when least expected, it had suddenly ended. Tragically. Having your husband killed in a hit-and-run accident meant Jasmine had never taken anything for granted again. Moving to Samphire Bay and renovating her cosy, flint-stoned cottage by the sea had been her salvation. Meeting Robin had more than been her salvation. He was her second chance at happiness. Having Jemima and Barny had been the ultimate icing on the cake.

So, yes, their wedding/christening would be different, but every bit as significant – another precious milestone in life.

'Right, that completes the guest list then,' said Robin, interrupting Jasmine's thoughts.

'OK. We'd better get the invites sent pretty promptly,' she replied, ever mindful of the looming date. They both wanted a wedding before winter crept in, which meant speedy planning. Hopefully September would still give them decent weather. They'd booked the church and gained permission to erect a marquee on the village green to celebrate afterwards. It was set to be a real village occasion for Samphire Bay.

Both sets of parents were at fever pitch. Jasmine's were obviously overjoyed to see their daughter settle down again after such a family catastrophe. The grandchildren they'd been blessed with were an absolute delight. As for Robin's parents, they were just plain relieved their son had found such a gem in Jasmine, especially after the scheming ex-girlfriend he'd had, who'd completely taken him to the cleaners. No doubt this wedding and christening was going to be celebrated to the max.

—

When Robin and Jasmine approached Tara about being a Godmother, she'd been so touched, if not a little surprised.

'Of course we want you to be Godmother, Tara. We'll never forget how you saved the day,' Robin had told her.

Jack had looked at her bemused, never understanding why she was so modest. I mean, who else would they have asked to be Godmother when she'd helped to practically save their babies' lives? To him, Tara really didn't comprehend how special she was; and he was beginning to understand why. Richard. That prick of an ex-husband of hers. He'd robbed her self-worth, taken her spirit. Not only that, but something else had been bothering her of late. Since the other day when they'd had such a lovely time chilling at his house, something had happened. He could tell. He'd wanted to broach the subject, but couldn't as they'd arranged to meet Robin and Jasmine in The Smugglers. What he needed was Tara on her own, preferably in her own surroundings where she'd feel most relaxed. It had been good to meet Robin and Jasmine, as they'd had lots to discuss, but he couldn't help feeling that Tara had been somewhat occupied, as though her mind was elsewhere.

Jack was also concerned about Calum. He often remembered their talk when he found him smoking on the beach, and how resentful he'd been. How did he feel now? And would he hide it from Tara? She certainly didn't know he smoked. Fortunately, after meeting at

The Smugglers, Tara had provided him with the perfect opportunity to find out.

'Why don't you come to mine for dinner this weekend? I've got Calum and I'm sure he'd like to see you.'

'Love to,' he replied, smiling. One way or another he'd find out what exactly was going on. He suspected Tara was in a vulnerable position and it was killing him.

Chapter 38

Jack entered the Augusta House car park after being buzzed through. It was a warm, balmy evening, so he'd driven with the car top down. From the balcony of Tara's apartment, he saw Calum watching and waved up at him. Calum gave a cheery wave back, clearly pleased to see him. Jack felt a touch reassured, hoping tonight's dinner would go well. He'd brought a bottle of coke as well as wine with him, eager to include everyone.

Calum answered the door with a wide smile.

'Hi, Jack, come in. Mum's stressing in the kitchen,' he joked as Jack followed him inside.

'I'm not stressed!' called Tara, vigorously stirring a pot, red in the cheeks.

Jack laughed, thinking it was the first time he'd ever seen her flustered.

'She hates cooking, don't you, Mum?' teased Calum.

'Oi, you, less of the cheek.' She grinned, putting the pot in the oven. After closing the door and checking the oven temperature, she breathed a sigh of relief. 'Time for a drink,' she said.

Jack laughed again. It amused him how she looked more comfortable in A&E than in a kitchen.

'Here.' He passed her the wine. Then he turned and offered Calum the bottle of coke. 'Fancy some of this?'

'Yeah, thanks, Jack,' replied Calum, taking it off him. Tara went to the fridge where the prosecco was chilling.

'Let's start with this,' she said popping the cork.

'Hmm, something smells good,' commented Jack, making Calum giggle.

'Yeah, right,' he muttered with mirth.

'Hey, you, I've made my signature dish tonight I'll have you know,' Tara told him with faux indignation.

Jack smirked at the banter between mother and son, reminding him of his own mum.

'So, cooking's not really your forte then?' he asked with a grin.

Calum snorted. 'You could say that.'

Tara's eyebrows raised. 'I'm not that bad, but thanks, Calum.'

'What are we having tonight?' Jack asked, leaning against the kitchen worktop, winking at Calum.

'Chicken curry,' she announced proudly.

'With half chips, half rice,' added Calum.

'Ah, my favourite,' lied Jack to an unconvinced Tara and Calum.

Truth be told, Tara was a little apprehensive about tonight, especially knowing how good a cook Jack was. And yes, whilst Calum had exaggerated her lack of skill in the kitchen, she had to admit, she didn't enjoy cooking. Not one bit. She hated having to think, prepare and make a meal. It just bored her. She lacked the imagination and incentive to rustle up something different every day. Usually, after a hard shift, she'd opt for the quick and convenient option – bangers and mash was a staple meal. Luckily, Calum liked it too. Tara did, however, appreciate being cooked for and had thoroughly enjoyed Jack's creations. She loved his enthusiasm for producing good food, how he moved with ease about his kitchen, never ruffled.

'Dad's a good cook,' stated Calum casually whilst pouring himself a coke. Jack's eyes met Tara's. 'Mel's crap though,' he continued, making them exchange a smothered snigger. He looked up at Jack. 'Game of Gran Turismo?'

'Yeah, if we've time?' He glanced at Tara.

'Sure, dinner will be ready in half an hour,' she replied, glad that Calum had asked Jack to join him on his PlayStation. He was obviously comfortable with him and this pleased her.

Whilst busy in the kitchen, Tara could hear cheers and shouts of laughter coming from her son's bedroom. It had been a while since she'd heard that. Once the curry was ready, she popped her head around the door to see both Calum and Jack intensely operating their hand controllers, eyes fixed on the screen. Calum's tongue was sticking out the side of his mouth in concentration.

'It's ready,' she said.

'Just a minute, Mum,' replied Calum, not taking his eyes off the game.

'Come on, buddy,' nudged Jack.

Reluctantly Calum gave in and they were soon sat at the table eating.

'This isn't too bad, Mum,' remarked Calum tucking into the curry.

'Thank you, Calum,' replied Tara dryly.

'It's lovely,' said Jack smiling at her.

'What's for afters?' asked Calum.

'Cheesecake, your favourite,' replied Tara.

Calum turned to Jack with a cheeky wink. 'Shop bought, not homemade.'

'Oh, give your mum a break,' he laughed. Then added, 'She's an amazing doctor you know. Excellent with a needle and thread.' He lifted his hand to show Calum the scar he was left with from the wound that Tara had stitched.

'Wow,' said Calum staring at it. 'Does it hurt?'

'Not now, thanks to your mum,' replied Jack.

'That's how you guys met, isn't it, the hospital?'

'It is. I sliced my hand on a window I was installing and was rushed to A&E.'

Calum's eyes slid from Jack to Tara, as if for confirmation.

'Yes, and I—'

'Came to the rescue, again,' cut in Jack.

Tara looked at him and smiled self-effacingly. There it was again, he thought, her modesty. He got the impression Tara never gave herself the full recognition she deserved.

'So, you see, your mum might not be the world's best cook, but she's a superhero to many.' He looked steadily at Calum, keen to drum home the message.

Calum shrugged. 'Yeah, I guess so.'

After eating, they watched an action film which Calum picked. Tara was reminded of happier times when they'd been a family with Richard. Most weekends had been spent this way. That thought inevitably led to darker ones, mainly the letter she'd received from him.

'You OK?' whispered Jack, sensing her unease.

'Fine,' she replied with a tight smile.

Once the film was over, Calum announced he was off to his room, leaving Tara and Jack alone. Jack seized his moment.

'Tara, what's troubling you? And don't say nothing,' he quickly added, seeing the beginnings of her denial.

He could tell by her expression she was about to deny anything was wrong.

Tara let out a heavy sigh.

'Perhaps it's easier just to show you,' she replied somewhat wearily.

'Show me what?' frowned Jack.

Tara got up and retrieved Richard's letter from her bag.

'This,' she said, handing it to him.

Jack scanned over the printed words, his jaw tightening all the time. A slow anger built up inside, threatening to spill out.

'Do you want me to speak to him?' he asked in a low, controlled voice.

'And say what, Jack? Not that he'd listen to anybody, especially you. Apparently, according to that,' she said and tipped her head towards the paper Jack was clutching, 'you're my *young beau*.'

'*Young*? I'm only two years younger than you, for God's sake,' spat Jack, clenching his fist.

Tara nodded. 'Which makes you several years younger than him. He'll hate the fact he's older than you. Richard's a vain man.'

'And a jealous one,' retorted Jack.

'Absolutely. He too has now been replaced by someone younger. He's also had a financial knock, which must sting, because he's also materialistic.'

'He's lashing out, trying to hurt you,' said Jack in disgust.

'That's what Claire said.'

'She's right. I mean, all this threat of full custody… Does Calum even know?' he asked, faced etched in concern.

'No. There's been no mention about this at all. And I refuse to discuss it with him.'

'I don't blame you. It's just going to disrupt his world. The *selfish* bastard,' he cursed under his breath, fury rising further. 'What does Claire advise?'

'To be honest, I don't think she's taking him seriously. She says to wait for a solicitor's letter, then act.'

'You mean you could end up in court again?'

'Yes, we could, because there's no way he's taking Calum from me,' she choked, chin trembling.

'Oh, Tara, come here.' Jack wrapped his arms tightly around her. Never had he felt such a need to protect.

Chapter 39

The next few days left Jack unsettled. Seeing Tara so upset was eating him up inside. The most frustrating thing was the feeling of utter helplessness, not being able to do anything about the situation she was in. Yes, he could offer words of kindness and support, but the real problem, Richard, he couldn't approach. He accepted it would only make matters worse. Jack respected Tara's opinion, and he agreed that speaking to her ex-husband would only antagonise him further.

So, here he was, hammering nails with force in an attempt to vent all his anger. He and Robin had almost completed the reconfiguration of the first apartment. Once all the dividing walls were up, they intended to use it as a template for the remaining five apartments.

Robin looked at his friend's expression, a furrowed brow and clenched jaw.

'Everything all right, mate?' he asked with concern.

Jack stopped what he was doing and put his hammer down. Staring Robin in the face, he gave a tired sigh.

'Not really, no.'

'Come on, time for a brew,' replied Robin reaching for his flask. He knew his friend was desperate to offload something. They propped up on a nearby windowsill and Robin poured them both a coffee. 'Right, out with it,' he said passing a cup.

'It's that prick Richard,' answered Jack witheringly.

'Tara's ex?'

'Yeah, Tara's ex,' came the flat reply.

'What's happened?' asked Robin, blowing on his coffee.

Jack shook his head, then went on to outline Richard's letter and his intention of applying for full custody of Calum. Robin sat in silence listening to his friend's dilemma.

'Poor Tara. She doesn't deserve any of this,' he said quietly when Jack had finished.

'Too right. And what really pisses me off is the way he's using Calum as some kind of pawn,' said Jack in disgust.

'Well, yeah, didn't he let Calum down the day of Felix's launch party?' asked Robin, remembering how Calum had arrived with Jack and Tara unexpectedly.

'Exactly. When it suits. He won't really want Calum full time. It's just a way to get at Tara.'

Robin nodded his head sadly in agreement. 'So, where does all this lead to?' he asked.

'Court, again,' said Jack in defeat. Just when he thought life had come good with Tara, they were now expecting another court hearing to loom over them. Then, a sinister threat struck him like a thunderbolt. What if Richard won? What if Calum was taken from Tara? It didn't bear thinking about. Surely, any judge in their right mind would see through Richard? Wouldn't they? A chill ran down his spine. My God, what must Tara be feeling?

'Listen, mate, it probably won't even happen. I can't see Richard being awarded full custody. I mean... why would he? It's not as if Calum's in any danger living with Tara, is it?' said Robin incredulously.

'Of course not, but it's still stressful being put through the court proceedings, having to prove yourself as a parent,' replied Jack taking a sip of his drink. He continued with narrow eyes, 'If anything, it's Richard who's the unfit parent, the way he just abandoned them *and* left Tara with hardly any money to live off. That woman's the one who kept it all together. Tara deserves a medal for what she's had to endure,' he finished with a raised voice.

'I know, I know,' appeased Robin, trying to calm him. In an attempt to help, he suggested having the couple over for dinner.

'Thanks, mate, but our hearts wouldn't really be in it. I don't think we'd be good company at the moment,' said Jack apologetically.

Robin nodded, understanding. He only hoped things would get sorted before the wedding and christening. The last thing they needed was a gloomy best man or downhearted Godparents. Robin wanted the occasion to be a celebration for all, *everyone* enjoying themselves. As if sensing this, Jack shook himself.

'Anyway, sorry to have dumped all this on you,' he smiled weakly.

'Hey, that's what friends are for. Remember when you gave good advice to me?'

He was of course referring to the time when he'd first met and fallen for Jasmine. Robin had been wary of letting her know his true feelings, especially as she'd only just become a widow. It was Jack who had given wise counsel, telling him to lay his cards on the table and that he'd know when the time was right to do so. And he'd been absolutely right. Robin had done exactly as his best friend had directed, and it had been the best course of action he'd ever taken in his life. Look where it had led him.

Wanting to inject a degree of optimism into Jack, he nudged him. 'Don't worry, mate, it'll all come good, you'll see.' He looked searchingly into his face.

'Hope so, Rob. I hope so,' replied Jack.

—

Meanwhile, Tara's friend, Claire, was also endeavouring to install confidence.

'Have you received anything from Richard's so-called solicitor?' Claire asked over the phone. She used the words 'so-called' as she was still unconvinced Richard had actually appointed one, especially 'one of the best' as he put it. To Claire, that meant real money, and if there was one thing she knew about Richard, it was his reluctance to part with it. No, he was merely trying to frighten and upset Tara, and, judging from the way her friend was reacting, it was working.

'No, not yet,' replied Tara. 'But that doesn't mean a letter won't arrive imminently,' she added in a fretful tone.

'Well, let's face that if and when it does,' countered Claire. 'I honestly think he's just trying his best to scare you, Tara. There's not a hope in hell he'd ever get full custody of Calum.' She spoke in a firm, assertive voice, adding conviction to her reply.

'But, what if—?'

'Don't start the "what if" game, please, Tara. That's exactly what he wants, to mess with your head.'

Tara closed her eyes, wishing the whole thing would just vanish from her plagued mind. Claire was right; Richard wanted her to be forever tormented instead of living a happy life without him. Or, more to the point, with someone else. And if that someone else was younger, handsome and fun around his ex-wife and son, well then he'd really up the ante – and he really had.

Since receiving Richard's letter, Tara had felt sick to the stomach. A constant anxiety spilled over her, quashing any hope of happiness. She'd cry into her pillow at night, hoping Calum couldn't hear her in the bedroom next door. Half of her expected Jack to end their relationship – and she wouldn't blame him if he did, what with all the baggage she had. Not Calum, obviously, but certainly a vengeful, spiteful ex-husband who was determined to ruin her relationship. Who would want that?

Tara now started to envisage living the life of a divorcee for ever, always waiting for Richard to come and destroy any second chances she may have. She imagined a deserted existence, alone and without Calum. At this point she started to hyperventilate. It had been a long time since that had happened. Her final exams and the day Richard admitted his affair had been the last time her body had reacted so violently. Tara's eyes frantically searched for a paper bag to help regulate her breathing. Speaking to Claire was increasingly stressful, and her chest was starting to tighten.

'Tara, are you still there?' asked Claire a little sharply.

'Yes… Look, I've got to go. We'll speak later,' wheezed Tara.

'Tara? Are you OK? Please, don't worry—'

Tara put the phone down, rushed to the kitchen drawer and pulled out a paper bag. Delving her head into it, she took great gulps of air. Watching the bag expand and deflate was therapeutic and soon her thumping heart subsided. Her body was regulating back to a calmer state. Would she *ever* truly be at peace?

Chapter 40

Bunty and Perry sat in deckchairs on the lawn, enjoying a cup of Earl Grey tea and the view before them.

'Ah, this is the life,' exhaled Perry, his hand shielding the sunlight. He gazed out to sea, watching the silver waves glimmer in the distance against a clear, azure-blue sky.

'It certainly is,' sighed Bunty in contentment.

When first moving from her childhood home to the old fisherman's cottage, she had worried about how life-changing it would be. But that worry had all been in vain. Both she and Perry had built their new lives together seamlessly in the enchanting, flintstone house, and still to have such stunning, panoramic views of the bay was an absolute God's send. Granted, the art deco house on the peninsula was undoubtedly in a prime location, standing prominently on the rocks with uninterrupted vistas, but even Bunty conceded it had been time to leave and start a new chapter. She had no regrets. None whatsoever.

Turning sideways, she glanced over at Perry, the one and only true love of her life. Yes, her old house was a huge, impressive place packed with timeless charm and character, but it didn't *completely* hold such happy memories within its walls. It contained good and bad recollections.

Then, just as she was reminiscing about her previous home, the current occupiers walked up the garden path.

'Emma!' cried Perry in delight, making Bunty's mouth twitch. She noticed Felix didn't get the same welcome.

'Hello, you two,' she said, rising from her deckchair to greet them both.

'Hello, Bunty,' replied Felix, kissing her cheek, then nodded towards Perry.

'Here, sit down, Emma, I'll fetch some more chairs,' directed Perry, then disappeared into the cottage.

'And I'll fix us some drinks. Felix, sit here.' Bunty tapped the back of her chair.

Soon they were all sat chatting, drinking Pimm's.

'Hmm, lovely,' said Emma closing her eyes and savouring the taste. Then, putting her drink down on the grass, she faced Perry and Bunty with a big beam. 'We've some wonderful news,' she gushed.

Perry's eyes darted to her left hand, preparing himself.

'Oh yes?' laughed Bunty, sensing the same as Perry.

'*Lady Scarlett Investigates* has been nominated for a BAFTA award!' trilled Emma.

Bunty's heart sank a little, wishing it had been news of their engagement. Perry's didn't. Their heads turned to Felix. Bunty was the first to speak.

'Congratulations, Felix, you must be delighted.'

Felix broke into a grin. 'I'm thrilled.'

'What's the nomination for?' asked Perry.

'The best drama series,' replied Felix, looking him in the eye.

'Isn't it fantastic? Felix's first shot at directing and his drama's been nominated for a BAFTA!' cried Emma.

'It is. Well done, Felix,' agreed Bunty, subsequently turning to Perry with an expectant look, eyebrow slightly raised.

Perry coughed. 'Err... Yes, well done, Felix,' he mumbled.

'So, the show's *really* going to get full exposure now,' continued Emma, almost at fever pitch.

'Does this mean your singing will too?' Perry swiftly cut in, ever mindful that his daughter's sweet voice had sung the theme tune to the show.

'Yes, Perry, it definitely does,' assured Felix, still looking directly at him.

'Oh, Emma!' Bunty clapped her hands together in glee.

Perry's eyes filled with emotion. His little girl was finally getting the recognition she deserved. All her life she'd longed for a singing career. Maybe now could be the big breakthrough?

'So, you may get a singing contract of some kind?' he tentatively asked.

'Hopefully!' exclaimed Emma, raising crossed fingers.

Perry looked at Felix for confirmation.

'I seriously suspect there's going to be a lot of interest from record companies,' he reassured, then squeezed Emma's hand.

'That's amazing news, Emma,' said Perry on the verge of tears. He got up to hug her. Bunty looked on with affection. Something told her that this revelation was far more pleasing to Perry than the one she'd wanted.

When voicing this later that evening, Perry had feigned puzzlement.

'Don't know what you mean, Bunty,' he frowned.

'Oh, come on. You know perfectly well what I mean,' she spluttered.

'What?' he asked, wide-eyed.

'Stop pretending, Perry. You thought, as did I, that they were going to announce an engagement.'

'Well…'

'You did, Perry. I saw your eyes flicker over Emma's hand, expecting to see a ring there,' she replied firmly, arms crossed over her chest.

'OK, yes, I suspected Felix may have popped the question,' he admitted, then added, 'but he didn't, did he?'

Bunty shook her head in disbelief. 'No, not on this occasion, but it's *highly* likely that he will at some point,' she countered, suddenly feeling a spark of irritation at Perry's attitude. Talk about déjà vu. Then, unable to stop herself, she spoke in a low, menacing tone. 'You know, you're beginning to remind me of someone.'

Perry flinched, immediately comprehending what she was insinuating. Hamish Deville, Bunty's manipulative, selfish, old bastard of a father, who had scuppered any chance of his daughter's happiness – was this who he reminded her of? Dear God, surely not?

'That's a touch harsh, Bunty,' he replied in a quiet voice.

'Is it? Is it really?' She looked straight at him.

'I'm nothing like your father,' Perry stated flatly.

'There's definitely shades of him in you, or at least there will be, if you don't change your attitude,' Bunty told him straight. 'What is it about Felix you resent?' she asked in exasperation.

'I don't resent him. He's always been good to Emma…'

'Then what is it?' Bunty asked, her voice a little calmer now, seeing the genuine confusion in Perry's expression.

'I… don't know. I'm just scared he'll…'

'He'll what?'

Perry blew his cheeks out. 'That he'll hurt her, I guess. It doesn't help that he spends so much time in London, leaving her in that big house all alone.'

'Like I was for years, you mean?' she replied with soft sarcasm.

'Yes. Exactly like you,' came the direct reply, making her blink. 'Only, unlike your father, I don't want that for my daughter. I want her to be cared for, looked after,' he raised his voice with passion.

'But Emma *is* cared for by Felix. He's a rich movie star, for goodness' sake!'

'It's not just about the money, Bunty,' he argued. 'It's about that someone who loves you, being there by your side, all the time.'

'Yes, and that someone who wants to marry you, to enable that to happen,' answered Bunty in a patient tone.

Perry, without realising it, had contradicted himself. Their eyes met.

'Am I being unreasonable?' He swallowed, the comparison to Hamish Deville still stinging.

'Only if I let you,' she laughed gently, glad he'd finally seen sense.

'Sorry.' He looked at her with doleful eyes.

'Oh, come here, Perrywinkle,' she teased, wrapping her arms around him. Then, pulling back she faced him. 'Listen, you are a loving, protective father and Emma couldn't have a better parent, but—'

'It's time to let go, let her live her own life, make her own choices and stop worrying,' he acknowledged dryly.

'Yes, you've finally got it.' Bunty gave the thumbs-up.

Chapter 41

Tara had collected her mail and was sifting through the various bills, flyers and leaflets when a thick, cream envelope made her jolt. The quality of the paper told her everything. This was 'the letter' she'd been dreading and even dared to hope would never be sent. But it had. It was right here, in her hand. On autopilot, she slid her finger through the seal and opened it. She quickly scanned the black typed writing, clearly and concisely outlining her ex-husband's intention to issue an application for full care and control of their son.

Tara's eyes widened in disbelief at the allegations Richard was throwing at her. He was basically insinuating whether, due to her work commitments, she was an ideal mother. He'd even gone so far as to question her reliability. He gave the example of when Calum had gone missing as evidence to support this.

She stared at the accusations Richard was making. Unbelievable – all untrue, trumped-up *lies*. But Richard already knew this. He was clearly playing dirty, using anything he could to twist and distort against her. The letter reiterated how he, his wife and future sibling to Calum would make a much more suitable family environment.

Tara sat down calmly and concentrated on her breathing, sucking air deeply in and slowly exhaling.

Richard was not going to win. He was *not* going to have any power over her. She was in control. Reading the letter again, once the shock had sunk in, she began to see it in a different light. This wasn't the instruction of a sensible, balanced client. It was spite from an angry, unreasonable, vindictive ex-husband. Pure and simple. So was Richard's revenge that he'd lost sight of what really mattered here. Calum. How on earth could you reason with someone like that? You couldn't. You had to fight fire with fire, and Tara was very prepared to do just that. The gloves were off. She rang Claire with the news.

'It's arrived,' she stated flatly, getting straight to the point.

There was a pause.

'Ri-ght… and what does it say?' asked Claire, obviously a touch taken back. She honestly thought Richard had been bluffing, that he wouldn't really have the gumption or inclination to pay a 'top' solicitor. No, it looked like the dickhead meant business.

Tara read out the letter word for word. The part concerning Calum's disappearance had Claire outraged.

'*What*? Calum left his friend's house, not yours. That could easily have happened on Richard's watch,' she scorned.

'I know,' agreed Tara, 'but it was on my watch, wasn't it? He's making it look like Calum didn't want to come back to me.'

'The prick,' retorted Claire with venom. 'Listen, don't panic.'

'I'm not,' replied Tara. She wasn't. If anything, she felt numb. Has it really got to this? she reflected sadly.

'So far, his solicitor has notified you of their client's intention to issue proceedings. They haven't yet formally made an application. No court hearing's been set.'

'So, what do I do?' asked Tara.

'For the moment I'll draft a letter in reply, respond with your intention to oppose any application made. Basically, I'll let them know we'll fight it all the way.'

Tara nodded. 'OK.'

'Then, we'll wait to see their response.' Part of Claire still suspected Richard was using scare tactics. It was one thing paying the fee for a solicitor's letter, quite another to have proceedings issued and representation in court. And for what? Did he really think he'd win full custody of Calum? Surely even he realised this was all bullshit? But still, at the end of the day, it was her friend who was hurting and, if anything (besides being a red-hot lawyer), Claire was a fiercely loyal friend. 'Has Calum said anything about this to you?' she asked.

'No. At least he's spared him that,' replied Tara.

There was a slight pause before Claire spoke.

'You'll have to tell him, Tara, especially if and when it goes to court. He may need to be interviewed.'

'You mean by a social worker?' Tara's chest started to tighten.

'Possibly. Depending on how far things get,' warned Claire in a sober voice.

'Right, we'll see how things progress first, then I'll sit down with Calum if needs be. That is, if Richard doesn't get there first.'

'But, as far as you're aware, he's not said anything to Calum yet?' checked Claire.

'No, I doubt it. Why? Do you think that's significant?' asked Tara.

'Hmm, could be. To me, it supports my theory that Richard doesn't fully intend to go through with all this. He merely wants to upset you.'

'Possibly,' conceded Tara.

'And how does he think Calum would react if he was told? He probably knows damn well Calum would kick up a fuss. There's no way he'd want to leave you and live full time with him and Melissa.' There was a brief pause before Claire asked, 'Does Calum even like Melissa?'

Tara let out a sigh. 'I'd say he resents her more than anything.'

'Exactly. That won't go down well if he's interviewed,' replied Claire with force. To her, this was all business as usual; for Tara, it was anything but.

—

Once more Jack was in turmoil, trying his best to think of a way to help Tara. Recalling how well the dinner with her and Calum had gone, he decided to return the favour and text her an invite.

> You and Calum fancy dinner at mine tonight?

> Yes. That would be lovely, thanks.

> 7p.m. OK?

> Great. Should we bring our cossies?

Came the reply, followed by a smiley face emoji.

> Why not?

Jack added a winking face emoji with a chuckle. He decided to have another barbeque, keen to spend as much time outside in the warm evening sunshine as possible.

Tara and Calum seemed on good form when they arrived later on. Clearly Calum couldn't wait to get in the hot tub, having stripped down to his swim-shorts early on.

'Came prepared then?' laughed Jack.

'Can I?' he asked eagerly, pointing towards it, bubbling away. It looked too inviting for him to ignore.

' 'Course you can,' said Jack, enjoying his excitement.

Tara mouthed, 'Thanks,' with a grateful smile.

'Here.' Jack passed her a cool glass of white wine. Boy, did she need this, she thought taking a gulp.

'You OK?' asked Jack, seeing her knock it back.

'Richard's solicitor sent me a letter today, confirming his intention to issue proceedings,' she told him.

Jack nodded. 'You thought he would though, didn't you?'

'Well, I half hoped he was making empty threats… but apparently not.' She shrugged and took another mouthful of wine.

The urge to punch Richard in the face rose up inside Jack. What he wouldn't do for ten minutes alone with that guy. Instead of telling Tara this, he asked, 'What does Claire advise?'

'She's drafting a reply, stating our intention to object. Then we wait to see what happens next. The ball's in Richard's court.' The ball always seemed to be in Richard's court. A flare of anger flickered inside her.

'Mum!' called Calum, waving up at her from the swirling water he sat in.

'Is it good?' she asked with a laugh.

'Awesome! Come and join me!'

Tara looked at Jack with a raised eyebrow.

'Let's,' he grinned.

'I'll just go and change!' called Tara.

Before long all three were splashing each other and giggling like hyenas. It was a much-welcomed relief, rather than mulling over what the future held.

Chapter 42

Robin and Jasmine's wedding and christening plans were pretty much complete. They'd arranged the date, church, venue, caterers, music and flowers. Robin and Jack had their morning suits, and the twins were set to look adorable in their christening gowns. The only sticking point, not that Jasmine had openly admitted, was her wedding dress.

It wasn't as if she'd been looking and unable to find the right one, because she hadn't been looking at all. The thought of walking down the aisle again in a big, white frock really didn't appeal to her. It just felt... wrong somehow. Jasmine was adamant that marrying Robin would be a total contrast to her first wedding with Tom.

Of course the fact the day was a joint event with the christening would make it different, but Jasmine didn't want any similarities at all – and a white wedding dress was indeed a similarity. But what to wear instead? That was the question she'd been asking herself daily and still hadn't come up with an answer.

Not being able to discuss this with Robin, for fear he might take offence, she ran it past Bunty again. After explaining her quandary, Bunty nodded, understanding her friend's dilemma.

'Maybe just pick a totally different style of dress then?' she'd suggested.

'It would still be white though, wouldn't it?' replied Jasmine.

'Not necessarily. You can wear whatever colour you want,' reasoned Bunty.

'You mean have one made especially for me?' asked Jasmine, rather liking the idea of not having to choose a traditional gown from a bridal shop, or go online and try to pick one from the hundreds displayed on various websites. To her, they all looked the same and nothing particularly stood out. Jasmine was beginning to wonder how she'd managed to ever decide on one years ago, but then she'd been in a very different state of mind – a young, excited bride-to-be. Now she had experienced the trauma of losing her first husband and was a mother of two. Nevertheless, it *was* Robin's wedding too, and he was more than excited for the pair of them. Not that Jasmine wasn't excited, just more reflective. She was glad they were making vows together and having Barny and Jemima christened. To her it made their family complete.

'Yes,' answered Bunty, 'you could describe exactly what you want and get a dress tailor-made.'

'But that's just it, Bunty, I don't know what I want. Only what I *don't* want,' sighed Jasmine.

Bunty gave her a sceptical look. 'You must have some idea,' she said despairingly.

'Well...' began Jasmine. Bunty leaned forward keenly.

'Yes?'

'I had thought maybe a suit of some kind, with a jacket?'

'A suit? We've been through this before, Jasmine,' cried Bunty, rolling her eyes. She'd already given her opinion on that, stating her friend didn't want to look like some kind of executive.

'I know, but listen, hear me out,' replied Jasmine, then reached for a nearby magazine. She leafed through the pages until finding a photograph of a model wearing a military drummer-style jacket. It was red velvet with gold braiding across the front, had brass buttons and elaborate embroidery on the sleeve cuffs. Bunty's eyes narrowed, taking it in. She paused before answering, wanting to choose her words carefully.

'I love the military style…'

'But?' prompted Jasmine, sensing there was definitely one coming.

'The material. Red velvet? Really?'

'Hmm, I know what you mean,' agreed Jasmine. Then added, 'What about pale pink silk?'

Bunty's face lit up.

'Yes! That would go beautifully with the gold braiding and embroidery!' she cooed.

Jasmine gave a huge beam, which soon dropped at seeing Bunty's raised hand.

'But not the jeans,' she insisted, pointing to the model's boot-legged denims, making Jasmine throw her head back in laughter.

'I wasn't thinking of wearing jeans!' she exclaimed.

'Wouldn't put it past you,' replied Bunty deadpan.

'Don't be daft,' retorted Jasmine.

'Well, what would you wear the jacket with then?'

'A skirt. A matching long, silk skirt. I'll even wear gold ballet shoes. How does that sound?' She looked her friend in the eye and was rewarded with a nod of approval.

Bunty smiled. 'Perfect. That sounds absolutely perfect.'

So, now that Jasmine had finally decided on what to wear, the race was on to get it made. Bunty had asked Emma for any recommendations. Luckily, she knew of a highly skilled seamstress in Lancaster. And, Bunty being Bunty, had leaped on the opportunity.

'We'll all go into Lancaster together!' she'd cheered, eager for a girly day out. This time Jasmine was more than happy to go along with her friend's suggestion. She was also pleased that Emma would be coming too.

Robin was just plain relieved that Jasmine seemed to be more relaxed. She no longer appeared angst about the whole thing.

'Looking forward to today?' he asked when the dressmaker's appointment came. He was to drive everyone into Lancaster and pick them up later.

Jasmine grinned. 'Yeah! Now I know what I'm wearing, I can't wait.'

'Good.' He lowered his head and kissed her lips. 'Have a great time and don't worry about us,' he teased, thumbing behind him to where the twins lay fast asleep in a Moses basket. Jasmine peeked into it and her heart melted at seeing Barny and Jemima holding hands side by side.

'Aw, look, Robin,' she whispered.

'I know.' He gave a soft chuckle, adoring the sight before him.

Jasmine, Bunty and Emma arrived at the dressmaker's late morning. After Jasmine showed the photograph of the model from the magazine and explained the material she wanted, her measurements were taken and further appointments were set. This left the rest of the afternoon for lunch and drinks. Plenty of drinks in fact.

'Bubbles!' announced Bunty on entering the nearest pub. 'This calls for bubbles!'

'Hear, hear,' agreed Emma, striding to the bar with purpose. Jasmine loved their gusto and *joie de vivre*. It was infectious. It also solved another quandary: a hen do. She hadn't arranged one, for the simple reason she didn't want one, not when having to tend to twins around the clock. Instead she'd relish every moment today, fully intending to make the most of it.

'Oh yes, definitely. Crack open a bottle!' she chimed.

'That's my girl,' said Bunty with a nudge.

Emma returned with champagne in an ice bucket and glasses, while Jasmine and Bunty were perusing the menu. After pouring them each a glass, she raised hers.

'To you, Jasmine, and your wonderful wedding outfit!'

They all clinked glasses and took a gulp of fizz.

'Hmm, that tastes divine,' groaned Bunty, who was more than ready for a drink. It was tiring work listening to every minute detail and description of a rose silk military jacket and matching full skirt. Still, if it made her friend happy, then it was worth the wait.

'What time's Robin coming?' asked Emma, hoping for a session. It had been a long time since she'd got bladdered in Lancaster. And she never thought she'd ever think that.

'When we're ready,' Jasmine laughed, in no hurry to rush home either.

'That's my girl!' repeated Bunty in delight.

Chapter 43

The next day left all three ladies with horrendous hangovers. Perry, who found it most amusing, announced he was going to visit his daughter.

'I'm off to Emma's. You OK?' he asked, smirking at his wife.

'No, and I don't think Emma will be either,' came Bunty's flat reply.

However, when he reached the house on the peninsula, it was Felix who answered the door to him.

'Perry, this is a nice surprise.' He welcomed him inside the hall, before telling him, 'I'm afraid Emma's in London.'

'London? Why is Emma in London?' he asked with a frown.

'I'm sure she would've wanted to tell you herself... But Laurence Willis, the music director for the drama, is introducing her to a record producer he knows, with the proposal of a record contract.' Felix gave a dazzling smile.

Perry's eyes widened. 'Really?' he gasped. Both men stood staring at each other for a moment, then Felix ushered Perry into the drawing room.

'Come through, I'll make us both a drink. Whiskey?'

Perry followed him and sat down awkwardly. Had he known Emma wouldn't be around, he'd never have visited. Being alone with Felix made him feel a touch uneasy.

'Whiskey would be great, thanks.'

As if reading his mind, Felix turned from the drinks cabinet to face him, looking like he needed to address something.

'I'm pleased we have this opportunity alone, Perry,' he said, passing him a cut-glass tumbler.

'Oh yes?' Perry took a sip of the ochre fluid and let the sharpness hit the back of his throat. He was glad of it.

'Hmm,' replied Felix taking the seat opposite him. He crossed one leg and looked frankly at him before continuing. 'Because I get the distinct impression that you don't really like me.' He stared him out, then added, 'And I'd like to know why.'

'It's not that I don't like you, Felix, but I'm unsure of you.'

'Unsure?' Felix frowned. This reply puzzled him. If there was one drawback from being in the public eye, it was the media attention he received. His personal life had been plastered all over every tabloid going. The world and its wife knew everything about him. He'd no secrets whatsoever. As far as Felix was concerned, he was an open book. What you saw was what you got, and surely he'd made it blatantly clear how much he cared for Emma?

'I mean… I know all's well with you and Emma at the moment, but you're a rich and famous actor, Felix, you could easily move on—'

'*Move on?*' cut in Felix incredulously.

'Yes. Emma's not as savvy as you. You're a good ten years older than her, with much more life experience… and…' Perry trailed off, not knowing what else to say, or how to express himself. He took another gulp of whiskey.

Felix sat forward intently.

'Listen, Perry, I may be a little older than Emma, but believe me, she's a very grounded, independent young woman. She knows exactly where she's going and what she wants. I'm here to love and support her in any way I can.'

Perry sat silently listening to him. Felix made good use of the chance to continue.

'Emma's in London today, about to sign a record deal, her life's ambition. I like to think I've played a part in that.'

Well, Perry couldn't argue with that, could he? If it wasn't for Felix's drama, Emma wouldn't have sung the theme tune, and she certainly wouldn't have been meeting a record producer today. It was all down to Felix.

'And as for *moving on*,' Felix almost spat the words, 'let me assure you, Perry, I've absolutely no intention of going anywhere. I'm here to stay, with Emma.' He stared him full in the face once more, almost challenging.

Perry rose an eyebrow. 'Fine words, Felix, but are you actually going to propose? Put your money where your mouth is?' It was time for some straight talking, to cut to the chase.

Felix didn't flinch. 'I already have,' he replied bluntly. 'But...'

Felix looked amused, pleased he'd managed to take the wind out of Perry's sails.

'She hasn't refused me, Perry, you may be pleased, or not, to hear. But she's asked for time. Time to make it in the music industry as Emma Scholar, not as Felix Paschal's wife.' He sat back somewhat smugly at seeing how shocked Perry appeared. 'So, you see, it's me dancing to Emma's tune. She's the one in control,' he finished.

Game, set and match to Felix Paschal, thought Perry. He had to hand it to the man, he had poise – but then he would have, every word he said being true. Emma *was* grounded, independent and now, after hearing the way she'd postponed Felix's proposal, a very prudent woman. He felt humbled. Extremely humbled.

'Well, it seems I owe you an apology,' he said in a quiet voice. 'I've clearly misread you Felix, and for that, I'm sorry.'

Felix gave a smile. 'No need to apologise, Perry. Just glad I've set your mind at rest.'

He nodded. 'And you have, definitely, thank you.'

'So, you've plenty of time to work on your speech,' joked Felix, keen to ease the tension. Christ knows how that's going to pan out, he thought. Looking at Perry now, he was clearly an over-emotional father. Or maybe that was normal? He'd never really known his dad, having lost him when he was very young. As for his mother, well, she was a no-nonsense French woman who called a spade a spade, no sentimentality there. She was, however, fiercely protective of him, so he did understand Perry's point of view.

'When's Emma back?' asked Perry, changing the subject.

'Tonight. I'm collecting her from the station at seven thirty.'

Perry hesitated for a moment. 'Maybe let her tell me about the record contract? Don't let on you've already told me?'

'As you wish,' agreed Felix with a nod of his head.

'Right… I'll be on my way then.' Perry stood and offered his hand. Felix shook it firmly. A fresh understanding had been formed.

Later that evening, as predicted, an extremely excited Emma rang Perry with her news. He smiled proudly at hearing of her up-and-coming record deal and all the trappings that would bring. Good for her. His girl, his little Emma, had finally made it in the music world. She was about to fulfil her lifelong ambition.

Bunty was also delighted to hear of Emma's success. 'Oh, Perry, that's amazing! Emma's about to become a star!' she exclaimed.

'She's always been a star to me,' he choked.

Chapter 44

Claire stared dumbfounded at the document before her. So, he really did mean business. Richard, true to his word, had actually filed an application for full care and control of Calum. Now it was her job to instruct her client, Tara. Or, in other words, tell her friend the news she'd been dreading to hear. Not wanting to do this over the phone, she texted Tara to ask if she was free that evening. She was. Claire hadn't enquired if Calum would be there, eager not to raise any apprehension. If he was there, he'd no doubt be in his bedroom playing music anyway, so she'd still be able to talk to Tara in private. Although, as things had now progressed to this stage, Calum would need to know of the proceedings in any event. What a bloody mess. And an unnecessary one. Did Richard honestly believe he would win? How could he? Either way, she'd make damn well sure he'd be the one footing the costs of all this nonsense.

Tara knew why Claire was calling and had been mentally preparing herself. Luckily, she'd been preoccupied for most of the day at work on the ward. A calmness filled her; she felt ready and determined to take on the world. When things hit rock bottom, the only way was up. But she hadn't hit rock bottom, a voice inside told her, and she was going to fight Richard and win.

Not for the first time, she wondered how it had got to this. Richard trying to take their son from her. The same inner voice gave her an answer. It had got to this stage because Tara, for the first time ever, had challenged him. She had fought for the financial settlement she'd deserved, and not only that, had gained a younger, handsome boyfriend in the process. Richard didn't like losing. He certainly didn't like the idea of Tara being comfortably well-off, or happy. And for the first time in a long time, Tara had been happy. Was it all about to come crashing down? Would Calum be wrenched away from her? Would Jack want to hang around with all this upheaval in her life?

Tears filled Tara's eyes as she drove home from the hospital. Pulling into the Augusta House car park, she composed herself before entering the apartment to face Calum.

'Hi, love,' she said with a forced smile, trying to act normal.

'Hi, Mum. I'm starving. What's for tea?'

Eating was the last thing on her mind.

'Do you want to order yourself a pizza?'

Calum's face lit up. 'Yeah, great.'

An hour later, Tara poured herself a large glass of wine and watched Calum wolf down his takeaway. All the time she was waiting for Claire to arrive. When Calum had finished, he went straight to his bedroom to watch TV.

Tara heard the buzzer and let Claire into the car park. She soon arrived at the door.

'Hi, come in, Claire.' Tara couldn't help but notice how serious she looked. 'Calum's just in his bedroom.'

'OK, I'll start then,' said Claire, pulling out a set of papers from her briefcase.

'That's the application then?' asked Tara.

'Yes. I'll let you read it first, then we'll go through it together.'

Tara's eyes darted over the papers. It read exactly as she'd suspected, all clear, concise and complete bullshit. It was an insult that she'd even have to defend herself to it all. Claire looked on fully appreciating her sentiment.

'So, let me just get this clear,' said Tara sitting forward. 'Richard is accusing me of being an unfit mother. He's claiming Calum would be better off living full time with him and Melissa, and Calum may be dragged into the proceeding and be interviewed?'

'Yes, basically,' replied Claire.

'Oh, my God.' Tara closed her eyes.

'But, Tara, we'll fight him all the way. I've responded to the application opposing the allegations made and will deliver a strong defence in court. Just because Richard's issued an application for full care and control of Calum, doesn't mean he'll get it. I'll also be calling Melissa. I think it would be interesting to hear what she has to say about all this.'

'Yeah.' Tara gave a harsh laugh. 'I'm pretty sure this wasn't part of her plan.'

'Exactly,' replied Claire forcefully, then quickly turned her head at seeing Calum enter the room. 'Oh, hi, Calum.' She gave a bright smile.

'Hi, Claire.' His eyes darted between her and his mum.

Tara swallowed nervously. Had he heard them talking?

'Everything all right, love?' she asked.

'Yeah,' he replied, walking straight to the fridge to pour himself a coke. 'What's that?' He pointed to the paper in Tara's hands.

'Oh, just some conveyance work that Claire's been doing for me, to do with buying the apartment,' lied Tara.

Calum looked unconvinced.

'Right, I'll leave you to it. See ya, Claire,' he called over his shoulder and went back into his room.

Tara and Claire exchanged a look.

'You're going to have to tell him, Tara,' hissed Claire in a low voice.

'I know. I will.'

But there was no need. Calum had heard every single word, and what's more, he was about to take matters into his own hands. He was fed up with being treated like a kid. He was fifteen in a few months. It was about time *he* made the decisions.

The next morning Tara woke with a heavy heart. All the emotional trauma was building momentum. It didn't help knowing she'd have to tell Calum everything either. Upon seeing his pale face, she wasn't surprised to hear he was feeling unwell.

'I feel sick,' he complained, then returned back to bed.

Tara wasn't working that day, so was happy for him to miss school.

'I'll bring you some breakfast,' she called.

'Not hungry.'

Tara paused. Any suspicion she'd had of him hearing her and Claire last night started to rise. She decided to let him sleep, hoping he would feel better in a few hours. Luckily, Calum did seem better when he woke later.

'Fancy something to eat now?' asked Tara. 'Something nice and light?'

'Yes, please. Can I have egg on toast?'

'Sure, coming up.'

They ate together with the radio on in the background.

'You're not going anywhere today, are you, Mum?' asked Calum.

'No. Why?'

Then there was a knock at the door. Tara frowned and went to open it. There stood Richard.

'Richard? What are you doing here?'

'I was summoned,' he replied.

'What?'

'By Calum.'

'But...' Tara turned to look at Calum who was watching her.

'Let him in, Mum.'

She blinked and stood aside.

Richard and Tara looked at each other, wondering what exactly was going on. Calum stood up from the breakfast bar.

'I want you both to sit down and listen to me.'

As if in role reversal, Tara and Richard sat down silently side by side and stared up at Calum, waiting for him to speak.

'I'm not stupid and I'm not a kid. Dad, I know you're trying to get me to live with you.'

'Well... now listen, Calum,' started Richard.

'No, *you* listen, Dad,' cut in Calum, 'I'm *not* living with you and Melissa. I'm staying here, with Mum. The arrangements are staying the same. I'm happy with them. And you can't tell me what to do, or how I feel. I'm not "little Cal" any more,' he finished with a hard glare.

Richard shifted uncomfortably. Tara resisted the urge to punch the air. She turned to face her ex-husband, waiting for his reaction, preparing for the onslaught. To her amazement, she saw a teardrop run down his cheek, then another and another, until he crumpled into uncontrollable tears.

'Richard,' said Tara softly, putting a hand on his shoulder.

'S... sorry. I'm so... sorry,' he choked.

Calum looked on, seemingly unmoved by his father's reaction.

'Who to? Me or Mum?'

'To both of you,' he replied in a strangled voice, wiping his eyes, shoulders shuddering.

And there it was. The apology. Finally. Tara was speechless.

'I want you to stop, Dad. Stop hurting Mum.'

A charged silence hung in the air.

'Yes, I hear you, Calum,' nodded Richard and stood in defeat to leave. He turned before opening the door. 'I'll withdraw the application,' he said, then quietly left.

Tara opened her arms and Calum rushed into them. Holding him tightly, she'd never felt so proud of her boy, who'd suddenly become more a man in both his parents' eyes.

Chapter 45

'Ready?' asked Robin with a warm smile.

Jasmine nodded and quickly kissed his cheek. 'Ready.'

Holding a baby each, they gently walked down the aisle. Barny and Jemima looked angelic in their christening gowns and almost bemused at the people lined up in pews staring at them.

There was indeed a lot for the congregation to take in – Jasmine, radiant in pale pink silk, complete with a gold-braided military-style jacket, and Robin, handsome and smart in his grey morning suit. Down they all came, slowly and serenely, a family of four, about to be christened and married.

Jack and Tara stood by the ancient stone font, waiting to take their roles as Godparents. Tara, however, only had eyes for Jack, who looked stunning. It was the first time she'd seen him so formally dressed and couldn't help but admire his broad shoulders and long, solid legs in a tailored suit. He caught her watching him and gave a cheeky wink. He too was having similar thoughts, appreciating Tara's svelte figure in the emerald-green wrap-over dress, which complemented her eyes. It was good to see some sparkle in them. Then he turned to face his best pal, Robin, who he hadn't seen so happy before. Joy practically oozed from every pore in his body. And as for Jasmine and the twins, pure beauty, in every sense.

Bunty sniffed with emotion at her first glimpse and grabbed Perry's arm. 'Oh, look at them,' she whimpered in awe. Perry patted her hand affectionately, thinking it wouldn't be long before he'd be making the same trip up the aisle with Emma. He stole a glance at his daughter, standing by the side of the alter with a microphone. She was to sing 'Seasons of Love'. Robin and Jasmine didn't want a soppy, loved-up, couplie song, but something upbeat for the whole family. Felix was nearby, sitting discreetly at the end of a pew, not wanting to attract any attention.

The church was packed to the rafters with all from Samphire Bay. It was set to be a real village event. The priest welcomed everyone, then guided Robin and Jasmine to join Jack and Tara by the font. The twins were to be christened first, before they exchanged wedding vows.

As the Holy water trickled over the babies' heads, Barny and Jemima wriggled in confusion, soon to be soothed by their doting Godparents. Once baptised, Jack handed Barny over to Jasmine's mum and took his place as best man next to Robin at the altar.

Jasmine's parents and brother looked on with tears in their eyes. Nobody could be happier for her, given the cruel circumstances she'd had to endure in the past. It was an overwhelming relief that she'd met Robin. Having the twins was the absolute icing on the cake. How life could change, literally within the blink of an eye.

Robin and Jasmine stood side by side as they promised to love and cherish each other, forsaking all others, till death did they part. Jasmine gulped at the words. Robin immediately took her hand and gripped it tightly. Never was there a more poignant moment. An emotional silence hung in the church, which was soon interrupted by the twins' cries, who'd had enough of all this and wanted to be comforted by their parents. A gentle laughter filled the air as Robin and Jasmine turned to them, then each other with a knowing grin.

When the priest announced them husband and wife, a huge roar came from the congregation, followed by a rapturous applause. The newlyweds collected their babies and set off back down the aisle.

Outside confetti was thrown, much to the elation of the twins, whose chubby little hands tried to catch. It all made for a spectacular, if not unusual, wedding photograph; a handsome groom with a stunning bride and two beautiful babes, eyes shining, all laughing in delight – a truly magical moment in time.

Everyone was greeted with champagne on the village green, where a huge marquee stood, covered with bunting and filled with long trestle tables carrying a lavish buffet. Emma's band sang and played live music, while the guests and villagers ate, drank and danced well into the evening.

Barny and Jemima lay tucked up snugly at home in their cots, being watched by grandparents. It had been quite an eventful day for them and the pair slept soundly. Meanwhile, their parents danced in each other's arms, gently swaying to the music.

'Happy, Mrs Spencer?' murmured Robin in Jasmine's ear. She looked up and smiled lovingly at her husband.

'Very happy, Mr Spencer.'

Chapter 46

The last of the summer days nudged into early autumn. As the nights drew in, a cool breeze rippled the shore of Samphire Bay. All the colourful flora that had once burst vibrant with life, faded into muted shades. Golden and bronze leaves swayed from branches, while the hedgerows withered, soon to decay. A still quietness hung in the air, as if bracing for the winter ahead. The sky still offered warm, amber sunrises, magnificent lilac-pink sunsets and indigo nights studded with bright stars.

Samphire Bay was an enchanting place, whatever the season or time of year, proving to be a haven for those who lived there. And nobody believed that more than Tara, who walked barefoot along its sandy coastline. She breathed the sea air in deeply, filling her lungs with its salty freshness. All was calm, both outside and personally within. She'd come full circle. From being the harassed, single mother, full time doctor and wronged wife, she was now a happy, loved mum, part-time doctor and partner to a caring, supportive man. Jack was compassionate, showered her in compliments, praised her, made her feel *good* about herself.

The last few weeks had taught Tara a lot. Mostly how much her son was changing. The mood swings were few and far between now, thank goodness. She was watching him grow, amazed at the rate puberty had kicked in.

He was almost as tall as her now, and his body was nowhere near the thin and lanky streak it had been. Calum was filling out, developing a physique and his voice had broken, making him talk deeper. Tara loved every inch of her boy who was maturing into a lovely young man. She was so, so proud of him. His brain as well as his body was ageing. Calum knew his own mind and wasn't influenced by anyone — something she and Richard had soon learnt. But she was glad. It meant their son couldn't be manipulated by his father. After all, it was Calum who had put a stop to his ridiculous attempt to take him away from her. He was also proving to be intelligent, gaining high exam results. Tara had been delighted when he announced he wanted to study medicine. Since then, Calum had remained focused, already shortlisting the universities he wanted to go to. Lancaster was at the top of that list, so it seemed he too had fallen under Samphire Bay's spell.

As Tara slowly meandered up the beach, she caught sight of The Cove, Jack's fabulous home. She smiled to herself, remembering the first time she'd seen it whilst out jogging. How much had changed since then. Their relationship was getting stronger by the day. It was important to her that Calum had also gelled well with Jack. The two shared a lively banter and they all rubbed along nicely together. Calum had even worked for Jack and Robin from time to time in the holidays. His strong build enabled him to shovel sand, mix cement and carry bricks.

Jack had been keen for Tara to blend in with his family too. After hosting a very elaborate dinner party for them all, Tara had been truly welcomed into the fold. Austin, in particular, had made a fuss, eternally grateful for her practically saving his life. Jack's mum couldn't do enough for her either. She clearly approved of the relationship and had high hopes for the future. Even Natalie, Jack's sister, treated her with an easy familiarity, often making each other laugh as the two shared the same sense of humour.

Then there was Richard. Tara gazed out to the still, slate-blue horizon and contemplated further. He'd changed too. Perhaps inevitable, given the fact he was now a dad again. And an older one at that. His daughter had made an early entrance into the world, being born prematurely at seven and a half months. Anastasia Aria (really?) had been the constant sole attention of her adoring parents. Calum fully expected to be roped in for babysitting duties given time, but didn't mind. Having a baby half-sister meant the pressure was off him, and she really was a sweet tiny tot.

Making her way up the shoreline, Tara turned into the cove that nestled Jack's house. The kitchen light was on, showing Jack busy preparing their evening meal. She marvelled again at his ease, overseeing pots and pans on the oven range, adding and tasting ingredients. As if sensing being watched, he suddenly turned and saw her through the window. He smiled and gave a wave. She waved back and made her way up the wooden steps inside.

'Hey, you,' he said, moving to kiss her.

'Hi. Something smells good.' She breathed in the delicious aroma coming from the oven.

'Creamy lemon king prawn linguine, with samphire, roasted tomatoes, spinach and capers,' he proclaimed with pride. He'd made a real effort, but then again, he always did. Jack loved having someone to cook for, and Tara was extremely appreciative of it. 'Pour us a glass of wine, will you?' he asked, checking a pan on the stove.

Tara went to the shelf for the wine glasses, where another framed photo stood, next to the one of Jack with his dad and sister outside The Cove. It was of them, holding their Godchildren, Barny and Jemima. Robin had taken it on their christening and wedding day. Tara couldn't help but smile at it. They looked good together, grinning up at the camera, cheeks touching. Who knows, maybe one day…

'Cheers.' She passed him his drink.

'Cheers,' he saluted. Their eyes met. For a moment they stood staring at each other. He could lose himself in those mesmerising green orbs in a flawless porcelain complexion. She was beauty personified, both inside and out. He was intoxicated. At least now she was beginning to recognise how special she was, well, certainly to him. Tara had developed a self-assurance and confidence he hadn't seen before. He hoped he'd contributed towards it. Both their lives had reached an equilibrium since meeting. He was content. For the first time in his life, Jack was happy to *just be*, no longer chasing the next thing, whether it be a work project or soulmate. He'd finally found it.

'What are you thinking?' Tara asked, taking a sip of wine.

'How wonderful you are,' he replied with a sexy smile. 'Come on, dinner will be ready in ten minutes. Let's go on to the balcony.'

They made their way out and stood overlooking the bay. Dusk was setting in and the last of the hot-pink sun was gradually disappearing, casting violet streaks across the sky.

'It's amazing, isn't it?' said Tara in wonder.

'It is,' agreed Jack, then turned to face her. 'Samphire Bay *is* an amazing place. It's a place of second chances and happy ever afters. I told you, didn't I, that everything would work out? Nobody's allowed to be sad in Samphire

Bay. It's against the law,' he told her, the corners of his mouth twitching.

'Yes,' she replied, wrapping her arms around him, 'a place of happy ever afters.' She held tight against his warm, solid body and blissfully closed her eyes.

Author's Note

I'm sorry this is my last visit to Samphire Bay and to say farewell to all the characters living there. It's been a pleasure to write about this idyllic seaside village in Lancashire, just tucked under the boarder to Cumbria. I based it on two places: Silverdale for its stunning coastline and Sunderland point for its peninsula cut off twice daily from the tide. Having travelled up its tidal road and walked along the peninsula, I got chatting to a lady who lived in one of the cottages there. It was fascinating listening to how they all lived around the tide and how it simply became a way of life. It struck me as rather quirky and I was inspired to write about it. They too held a Tea by the Sea event, which appears in the first Samphire Bay book. There isn't a Bunty Deville living there reading tarot cards, though!

I had to research the Art Deco period for this series and loved everything about it, the clothes, architecture, music and art, it's so stylish. From staying in Art Deco hotels and having cream teas in The Midland hotel, I've relished every minute.

I've particularly enjoyed the Samphire Bay series and dedicated all three books to family members, remembering those who have passed. I hope you've enjoyed these books too.

Bye for now,
With love,

Sasha x